"Here is a story about a rainbow of America's children working and playing together. Boy or girl, black or white, this book unifies us, and then teaches us about each other. This isn't a story just about sports—it's about life."

-Dr. Richard Lapchick, Director
Center for the Study of Sport in Society

"Young adolescents need to hear stories of feminine spirit . . . These characters resolve their differences with a refreshing degree of civility on the court. Their behavior off the court inspires, amuses, and reassures us that Maureen Holohan knows the game and is a master of her craft. *Friday Nights* will capture your heart and leave you craving more of Holohan's work."

-Christopher Papa
Language Arts teacher

"As I was reading *Friday Nights,* I was so pleased that a book with positive and realistic role models in a sports setting would be available for girls. It captures the essence of competition and also the realistic life lessons learned along the way."

-Kathy Chukas
A Sporting Chance Foundation

"The Broadway Ballplayers captures the essence of sports and their value to participants. These stories are important because they effectively translate from the viewpoint of the young female athlete the many lifelong lessons which sports can teach. We are happy to see a former Big Ten scholar-athlete make such good use of her athletic and educational experiences."

-Jim Delany, Commissioner
Big Ten Conference

Other books by **The Broadway Ballplayers**™

Left Out by Rosie

Everybody's Favorite by Penny

The Broadway Ballplayers™

FRIDAY NIGHTS

by Molly

Series by
Maureen Holohan

For information regarding permission, please write to:

The Broadway Ballplayers, Inc.
P.O. Box 597
Wilmette, IL 60091
(847)-570-4715

ISBN: 0-9659091-0-7

*This book is dedicated
to all of us who dare to dream
and play with passion.*

Don't ever stop.

Chapter One

Whenever I watched the sun lean down into the horizon of Anderson Park, I always made just one wish. I wished that somehow it could hold its spot in the sky a little longer for us than it did for the rest of the world. With the sun as our spotlight, the park was our stage. And I wanted to play forever.

Almost every day of the year, even during the bitter blizzards and scorching heat waves, we talked our way out of our small houses and apartments, and dragged little brothers and sisters down Broadway Avenue to the park. We played any and every game imaginable—tackle football, hide-and-seek, kick the can—and invented many of our own. A day rarely passed without one red-eyed kid going home with bumps and bruises, or another claiming that somebody cheated him or her out of a win. Very few of us openly reconciled after a heated argument, and never after a physical fight. But we didn't hold too many terrible grudges either. It wasn't anything out of the ordinary to see the same two kids celebrate a victory not too long after they had just finished slugging it out over something that seems silly now. But back then, it meant everything.

• • • •

It was a sizzling day in early June. Dozens of kids streamed down Broadway Avenue after school and brought life back to the lonely park. Some dragged their sneakers over the pebbles on the asphalt courts and others stirred up a dusty haze on the dirt field. Playful screams accompanied the sounds of laughter and excitement, which remained steady all afternoon.

"Next basket is point-game," Penny called out.

"Let's get this over with," Wil said as she grabbed her stomach. "I'm hungry."

"Don't worry," J.J. said. He threw his shoulders back and his chest out. "I'll end it."

Jeffrey "J.J." Jasper, who was the shortest kid in our class, always carried himself like a man three times his size.

"Trust me," he added, nodding his head, "it's over."

"Okay, shorty," I muttered.

"Try and stop me," J.J. shot back. He picked up the pace of his leisurely stroll, and started to pound the ball harder onto the blacktop. As I stepped up to guard him, I pushed back the loose strands of my curly auburn hair that fell out of my ponytail. I wiped away some sweat, which left dirt tracks on my freckled face. There was no way was I going to end the day with a loss.

After J.J. zipped the ball around to his teammates, it came back into his hands again. He swung the ball in front of me, and bolted toward the basket. When his wild running lay-up rolled out of the rim, I grabbed the rebound. I dished it to Penny and sprinted up the court.

"Don't let Penny loose!" J.J. pleaded as he ran back on defense.

J.J. had every reason to worry. Any kid who ever played at Anderson Park knew that when the game was on the line, Penny Harris was the player who usually ended it. Dressed in her matching headband and sweatbands, Penny looked as cool as she played. Eddie cut her off on the right and J.J. shut down her left. With nowhere to go, Penny twisted out of the double team and bounced the ball to me.

"Hit it, Molly!" she shouted.

My eyes didn't even see the basket. I grabbed the ball and tossed it up into the sky as fast as I possibly could. After I let it go, I cringed and begged for some miraculous roll or bounce. But my line drive didn't have a chance of falling through the iron.

Just before I threw a disgusted fit over missing, my eyes grew wide with hope. Penny had quickly maneuvered through the crowd, jumped up, and pulled down the rebound. One convincing shot fake left Eddie suspended and helpless in the air. Her eyes locked on the corner of the square and she smoothly and calmly let the ball go. It gently touched the aluminum backboard before it fell right through the net.

"Yes!" I screamed as I threw my clenched fists up in the air. I jogged over to Penny and reached out my hand.

"Way to go, P," I said.

"Good game," she added.

I went around to slap the sweaty hands of every player on my team. I was still smiling when I turned to J.J. His arms were like pipes at his sides. He clenched his fists and stomped the ground with one foot.

"Let's play to 15," he said.

"Nope," I said, snickering. "Nice try, J."

"Shut up, Molly," he said.

"You'll just lose again."

When his steely eyes got ahold of me, I realized that I should have just kept my mouth shut and walked to the water fountain like everyone else. J.J. was my friend in school and at the park, and I loved it when we were on the same team. But when we played against each other, we turned into different people.

"What's the matter?" he called out angrily as I walked away. "You scared to play some more?"

I felt two strong hands push my back and I flew forward. I whipped around and then stared down into J.J.'s scowl.

"Yeah," he fired back. "I thought so. You're so scared, you're shakin'." He started trembling and then leaned toward me and laughed right in my face.

"Don't be such a sore loser," I grumbled.

"You don't want to play because you're afraid you're gonna miss that shot again."

His words stung. "You know you'll miss again," he added.

The more he mumbled, the hotter my face turned. My bottom lip began to quiver.

"Shut up, J," I screamed as I jumped toward him. He dipped and then backpedaled away from me. I started running after him.

"Hold up," Penny said as she threw her arm around my shoulders. "Cut it out, Molly. It's over. Let it go."

I slowed down and took a deep breath. J.J. was too fast for me anyway. Chasing him around would have driven me crazy.

"See, there she goes again," he yelled. "Penny is always making your shots and bailing you out of trouble."

I raced through the list of comebacks in my mind, and came up with nothing.

"Why you gotta be like that, J?" Penny asked.

"She started it," he screamed. His eyes fell to the ground, and he began to walk away. No matter how many insults J.J. slung at me, nothing could erase the loss from his mind.

"You're just lucky, Penny," he grumbled. "Always so dang lucky."

"They don't call her Penny for nothing," Wil said lowly as she walked back onto the court.

Wil was right about that. Penny's grandmother nicknamed her granddaughter, and my very best friend, Shantell "Penny" Harris. She figured that everyone needed a bit of luck now and then, and this way, Penny would have it with her all the time.

All nicknames aside—which is a lot considering almost every kid on Broadway Ave. had at least two or three—the things that happened to Penny on any playing field had nothing to do with chance or a random good fortune. Pick it—basketball, soccer, football, softball—and Penny could play it. Most kids, including me, sounded like a herd of buffalo running down the floor. I claimed to be an expert on how not to get injured during my notorious crashes to the ground, but my black-and-blue knees betrayed me. I often wondered why such an amazing athlete like Penny hung out with a human floor mop like me. Especially after all the trouble my temper got us into. I had lost track of how many fights she had managed to talk me out of.

The day's last game at Anderson Park ended like most. The winners smiled excessively and the losers moped away.

"See ya tomorrow," Penny yelled with a smile to those who had enough for the day. "Same time, same place."

I picked up my ball and went right out to the spot in the corner where I had missed. I took one long look at the rim. I knew that if I made the simple shot then, I would only be kicking myself for not making it in the game. I shot it anyway. It was a perfect swish.

"Now why couldn't I do that in the game?" I mumbled.

"Don't worry, Molly," Penny said as she scooped the ball up from under the basket. "All that time you spend worrying about it makes you miss it. Just shoot it. And if you miss it, so what? Everybody misses."

Except you.

Wil hustled back onto the court wiping away the sweat that was running down her face. "Lemme get my last shot in," she called out just as Penny passed me the ball. I looked at Wil and kept dribbling.

"Come on, Molly," she whined. I smiled devilishly and made her beg some more.

"Come here, you punk!" Wil lurched toward me and took a swipe at the ball. I laughed at her and darted off. In two quick steps, Wil grabbed a hold of my shirt and started reeling me in. By then I was so weak with laughter, I just took the ball and shoved it into her stomach.

"Uhh!" she moaned.

"Well, you're the one who wanted it!" I called out with a smile. Wil just shook her head.

We rushed around trying to get in our last shot before we called it a day. But it was never just one or two. Just one more always turned into 10 and sometimes even 20 attempts. We flailed around the court, laughing and shooting and then chasing down the ball to do the same thing all over again. After one rebound, I started dribbling around to carefully decide where I would launch from next. I lifted my eyes up from my ball and they landed on my dad. He was dressed in his blue police uniform and was walking toward the court.

A stroke of panic swept over me. I was supposed to be home at 6 p.m. sharp.

"What time is it?" I blurted out.

Wil flipped her wrist and looked down at her watch. "Five fifty-six," she called out.

"Phew." I didn't want to hear it in front of all my friends about being late for supper. My fastest sprint home was one minute and 14 seconds. I had it covered.

"Hi, girls," my dad said, and then my little sister, Annie, sprinted out in front of him.

"Hi, Dad," I said smiling.

"Hey, Mr. O," Wil added as she walked over to pet my dog, Pooch, who was running around with his leash dragging on the ground.

"Hi, Annie," my friend Angel said to my sister.

Annie pushed her shaggy hair off of her forehead, and then smiled sheepishly as she skipped under the basket.

"Whatsup, Annie?" Penny reached out and slapped Annie five.

I felt like I had to say something, seeing how polite all my friends were to my little sister.

"Hi, skinny," I said softly so my father wouldn't hear. Annie's eyes narrowed and she scowled. She had one mean glare for a five year-old.

"Twerp," I added, making fun of her toothpick frame. Then I snickered. Annie bolted after me and tried to rip the basketball out of my hands. She was trying to prove to everyone that she was big enough and strong enough to hold her own at the park. I flipped the ball to Rosie and Annie slugged me in the stomach.

"Annie!" my father yelled. That was a warning.

"Molly's picking on me," she cried.

"That's enough," my dad said. "The both of you just stop."

Then he put his hands up for a pass, and Rosie fired one his way. Annie ran out in front of him and threw her arms up. His shot from deep in the corner hit nothing but air. It wasn't even close to the rim.

"I was fouled!" he cried.

"Yeah, right, Dad," I said.

The ball rolled away. Annie chased it down and passed it back to Rosie.

"I came down today because I wanted to let you know that I spoke with Mr. Freeman this morning," my father told us as Rosie's missed shot rolled his way.

The ball stopped bouncing and all eyes widened. Mr. Freeman was the Park District Athletic Director and was in charge of summer scheduling.

"Whadhesay, Dad?" I begged. He dribbled around, grinning. "Come on, Dad, stop teasing," I persisted. I reached out to steal the ball from him and grabbed onto his arm.

"First game is the Friday after school is out," he said.

"Ten days!" Wil quickly calculated.

"Yeah!" Penny cheered.

I jumped up and down. We had waited for what seemed like forever to hear about having the first summer basketball league for girls in the city. Now it was official.

"How many teams?" Penny asked.

"Six," my dad said.

"Only six?" I asked.

"How the heck are all the girls in the city supposed to play?" Wil asked.

"It's better than nothing," Angel said.

"That's right," my dad said. "You gotta take what they give you and then build from there."

"Are we all on the same team?" I asked.

"Well, there's one problem," he said and his smile disappeared. "It's only for girls going into the sixth, seventh, and eighth grades."

The celebrating came to an abrupt halt. All eyes fell on Angel, who was just finishing eighth grade. Her thick Italian hair was pulled back with an elastic band and a ribbon that she always tied in a bow. She picked up her green eyes, took a quick glance around, and then dropped her head to the ground.

Angel Russomano had moved to Broadway Ave. three years ago in the summer. The moving trucks hadn't even unloaded everything, and Angel had taken a jog down to the park. When we saw her coming, Wil, Penny, Rosie and I stopped shooting baskets and looked into the distance. A big white bow sat on the top of her head.

"Who's that?" Wil asked.

"The new girl," I replied.

Just before I made a comment about her bow and the pink outfit, I followed Angel's eyes down to the ground. A soccer ball was at her feet. Right then I knew that she was one of us.

Penny asked her to shoot some hoops, and she politely accepted.

"I'm Angela," she said, "but my family calls me Angel."

"Okay, Angel," I remembered my best friend saying, "I'm Penny."

From that day forward, Angel became the oldest member of our tight group of friends. So when my father told us that Angel couldn't play, we all took it hard.

"That's not fair," I mumbled.

"Are you sure she can't play?" Wil asked.

"Sorry," my dad replied. "All the kids going to high school have to try-out for the high school teams."

As much as we all didn't want to think about whether things would change next year, this was the first hint that it might be a little different without Angel around. There was an awkward silence.

"How about being an assistant coach, Angel?" my dad suggested. "You can practice with us."

Angel picked up her green eyes and took a quick glance around.

"Come on, Angel," Rosie said quietly. I turned to my short and wirey friend and was surprised to hear her speak up. "We need you," Rosie added.

"Well, OK, " Angel agreed. "But only if you all really want me to."

"You know if Rosie talks, it's important," Wil said. Everyone turned and chuckled at Rosie, who hid her eyes under her baseball cap. She smiled bashfully and shrugged her shoulders.

"It just wouldn't be the same without Angel's bony elbows flying all over the place," Penny joked, and everyone laughed.

"But coaches can't wear bows in their hair," Penny added with a smile.

"I won't," Angel said and she rolled her eyes. We always teased her about her bows and cute out-fits.

"What's our team name?" Wil asked.

"That's up to you," my dad replied. "We've got all the girls on Broadway."

"Well, it's gotta be the Broadway something," Penny said.

"How about the Broadway Stars?" Wil suggested.

Rosie and I liked it. "The Stars from Broadway," I added reverently.

"Nah," Penny mumbled. "That's too cocky. We don't want to sound cocky."

I stopped and thought for a minute. She had a point, considering that after her, we were really a bunch of scrubs.

"Who are we?" Wil huffed.

"Well, we're from Broadway and we love to play ball," Angel began. "Any kind of ball. Softball, soccer, basketball..." She paused. "How about the Broadway Ballplayers?"

"Sounds good to me," Wil said.

"Yeah!" Rosie added enthusiastically.

Our eager eyes then turned to the person who could make the decision unanimous.

"I like it," Penny said, smiling. "Good job, Coach." Angel's braces sparkled when she smiled.

"What do you think, Dad?" I asked.

Annie had backed him into the corner. He jumped up and settled in for a fade-away shot. It was all net.

"Yes!" he exclaimed. He pranced around holding his index finger high in the air.

"Lucky shot, Dad," I said. I chased down the ball and ran out to his spot. I used all my power and heaved the ball up. It clanged off the back rim, just like the shot I had missed in the game earlier.

Not again! I tipped my head back and searched the sky for answers.

"OK, Broadway Ballplayers," my dad said, "It's dinnertime and the Ballplayers have to eat! So let's get outta here. Finish up with your final exams and I'll see you at practice next week."

Chapter Two

I opened the gray metal box and flicked the switch. The fluorescent lights hummed, and then slowly began to brighten.

"Practices are here on Mondays and Wednesdays," said Mr. Harris. Penny's father and my father took turns managing and coaching all of our neighborhood teams. When they found out about this new summer basketball league, they re-worked their schedules because they both wanted to be a part of the league.

"Games are on Fridays," Mr. Harris said. "We'll let you know where they are each week."

"What if we can't make a practice or game?" Wil asked.

"Let us know as soon as you can," my dad replied. "We don't want to have to forfeit any games."

I picked at the string on the mesh ball bag as my father started to push the wide mop over the dusty floor. The top of the three-point lines at Lincoln School missed intersecting the center-court circle by about one foot. And the court was too narrow for the three-point line to reach the baseline.

"Any day now," Angel said with a smile. I pulled the last knot loose. I reached in and dug out one

basketball at a time. I threw three of them as far
away from Angel as I could. When there was only
one left, I wound up and Angel screamed, "Come
on, Molly!" I stopped and handed it to her.

"Just kidding," I said with a grin. Angel
snatched the ball out of my hands and I followed
her onto the floor.

"I don't understand why we have to go to school
tomorrow," Wil muttered as she dribbled. "It's not
like we're doing anything."

"It's like that every year," Angel added.

"We're going outside to play football during
math class and we're playing basketball all period
in gym," I yelled over my shoulder as I chased a
ball off the court. I walked within earshot of the
coaches, and suddenly grew curious. They were
talking in low voices. As I reached down for the
ball, I leaned toward them, and listened hard.

"I don't want them to get discouraged early,"
my dad murmured.

"I know," Mr. Harris said as he shook his head.
"The Hawks are so quick. And they're as big as high
school kids." My father's eyes fell upon me. I inno-
cently looked away, and then bolted back onto the
court.

"It's so dumb to have school when finals are
over," Penny admitted. "One more day and summer is finally here!"

"Did you find out how you did on the math
final, Penny?" I asked. I hated to keep the subject
on school, but I couldn't let my curiosity fester any
longer.

"I got an 85."

"Oh," I said, and my heart sank. I knew I shouldn't have asked. I felt so dumb.

"How'd you do?" Penny said.

"I got an 80," I mumbled.

"That's good," Penny said.

That wasn't good. It was awful. I actually thought I could get a 85 on the final, which would have placed me in the honors seventh grade math class with my best friend. But no matter how hard I tried, my best was barely a plain old fat "B."

"When do we get our report cards?" Rosie asked softly.

"Next Monday at conferences," Penny said. Then she looked at Rosie suspiciously. "You did all right, didn't you?"

Rosie shrugged. "I don't know," she mumbled.

"What'd you get?" I asked.

She shrugged again. This time her eyes shifted away.

All of us knew why. Rosie's older brother Rico barely got through high school. When he did graduate, he passed up college scholarships and moved on to professional baseball. A couple of weeks into practice, he injured his knee and was sent home. That was only part of the problem. The rest had to do with their father, who was one of the most intense parents I had ever seen. He was always all over Rosie's back about everything. I guess it was his way of making sure that Rosie didn't fall through the cracks, too. But she was already slipping.

"What's your dad gonna do?" Penny asked.

Rosie shrugged again.

"Wil," Angel asked. "how'd you do on your tests?"

"Good," Wil said softly, and then she shrugged. Penny always got good grades, but Wil was a genius compared to the rest of us.

"Have you ever gotten an A-minus?" I blurted out sarcastically. "Ever?"

Wil's eyes dropped to the ground. She turned and picked up a ball and then threw it up at the basket. My insides hurt after I realized what I had just done. When other kids in school made fun of Wil about her perfect grades, it was one thing. But it meant something else to her when we did it.

"Sorry, Wil," I said shamefully.

"That's all right," she mumbled. "What are you bringing to the pool party on Wednesday?" she said. The Lincoln "End of School Pool Party" was the buzz around the neighborhood.

"I'm bringing..." Angel started.

The whistle shrieked once, and we heaved up our basketballs. The annoying shrill of two more blows meant to hustle over. Quickly.

We jogged over. Actually, I was running fast. I almost tripped to keep up with Penny. Her calf muscles were like tennis balls in the backs of her legs. She practically floated across the floor. Angel and Rosie easily passed me by. But I could always count on coming in ahead of Wil. She was still panting as we stood at center court.

"Give me a week and I'll be running circles around all of you," she muttered.

Everybody laughed as the rest of our team filled in around the coaches.

"We're only going 'til 8:30 tonight instead of 9:00 because you girls have your last day of school tomorrow," my dad said. "So let's concentrate and work hard. Start with two lay-up lines."

We lined up for lay-ups, starting on the right. After about five minutes we took some jump shots. Then the whistle shrieked.

"Switch sides," my dad yelled.

The two balls bounced over to the dreaded left side. Using my weak hand was sheer torture for me. I tried to sneak in my right hand just for an extra measure of control. But like most times, as I put it, I was caught right-handed.

"Molly, use your left!" my dad called out.

"Ugh," I moaned softly to myself.

Wil dribbled in high with her eyes and glasses glued on the ball. Before she knew it, she was going up off the wrong foot, and too far under the iron rim. The ball ricocheted right back to her and bumped her in the head, which knocked her glasses off one of her ears. I burst out laughing, and then I scooped my hand over my mouth. But it was too late.

"Molly!" my dad yelled with a frown.

I shrugged and my eyes fell to the ground. He was right. I shouldn't have been laughing at anyone else. As comical as it was to watch what that left side could do to a person, I never thought it was that funny when it was my turn.

"Wrong foot! Keep your head up, Wil!" Mr. Harris hollered.

Feet, hands, right, left, wrong, head up. The simple lay-up drill began to tear at everyone's patience and spirit.

"I can't do it," Wil sighed.

"Shhh..." Angel hushed. "Don't let them hear you say that!"

"All right, that's enough," my dad said. "Let's break up for our shooting games. First team to 10 points watches the losers run a sprint."

"Yes!" Rosie cheered as she pumped her fist in the air. We all anxiously awaited our team assignment.

"Angel, Wil, Molly, Jen, and Rosie against Anita, Penny, Mary, Jess and..." Mr. Harris ran out of girls. He glanced around the gym.

"Sammy!" he hollered.

Little Sammy looked up eagerly, with the same brown eyes as his big sister. He dribbled coolly towards the basket, mustered all the strength in his pudgy six-year-old body, and shot the ball up. The ball softly bounced off the corner of the square and fell right through the basket—just like Penny had taught him.

"I'm on Penny's team, right?" he shouted.

"You got it," his dad assured him, knowing how much little Sammy adored his big sister.

We scurried around and arranged ourselves in a line on the right side of the baskets at each end of the gym. "Ready...Go!" yelled Mr. Harris.

"One...two...three..." Penny's team counted every shot they made. Our shots clanged off the rim and crashed off the backboard. The more baskets we missed, the more they made. Their shouts became incredibly annoying. My muscles began to tighten. I peeked down at the other end every couple of shots to see how far behind we were. Every time I did, I saw another shot singe the net. Even little Sammy was making more shots than me.

"Nine...ten!" they shouted in unison.

It began to sound like a broken record. Penny's team only lost one game. We lost five times.

"This isn't fair," Wil whined.

After our fifth loss, I was fuming. Penny hadn't even broken a sweat. She stood dribbling the ball back and forth between her legs and around her back. In her shadow was little Sammy doing the same exact thing.

As we all walked to the baseline, I glanced up quickly and caught Anita and Jess grinning smugly. I scowled and rolled my eyes back at both of them. It wasn't the running that bugged me. It was the losing. But for Wil, who stood next to me moaning, it was definitely the running that was causing her pain.

"I hate this," she grumbled as she waited for the whistle.

It was obvious that Wilma Rudolph Thomas was not going to grow up to be the track star her parents named her after. And she wasn't the most coordinated athlete around either. But she loved sports just the same, except when it came to one thing in particular: running.

"Show us some mercy, please," Wil begged dramatically. She pulled her sweaty T-shirt down over her tight shorts. Wil considered herself "big-boned," but kids in the neighborhood weren't so kind. After bending over to grab her knees, her blue-rimmed glasses slid down her nose.

"Come on, Mr. O," Wil whined to my father.

"This just stinks," I muttered quietly to Wil, hoping that empathizing would make her feel a little better.

"I've got a deal for you," Mr. Harris called out, and we all looked up eagerly. "If Rosie can step up here and make a free throw, you're all off the hook. No more sprints."

"Do it, Rosie!" Jen yelled.

"You got it, Rosie!" I cheered.

Wil clasped both of her hands together in front of her chin. "Please, please make it," she begged.

Without hesitation, Rosalinda Jones stepped onto the court, smoothly dribbling the ball in her right hand. This would have been quite a task for any ordinary 11-year-old. But "Rosie Jonzie," as we sometimes called her, was no rookie when it came to pressure. During some games and practices, Mr. Jones screamed and yelled at her so much on the sidelines, I wanted to cry for her. But Rosie never shed a tear. She was tough. She had to be. Her brother had been taking her to the batting cages since she was seven years old. After being thrown in the cages with smoking fastballs zinging by her nose, we all knew that it took a heck of a lot more than a free throw to rattle Rosie.

She flipped her long brown braid over her shoulder, and set herself on the line. A serious look washed away her sheepish grin. After a deep breath, she spun the ball out in front of her and dribbled four times. She eyed the basket, bent her knees and pushed the ball up off her fingertips. It went up. And up. It finally caught the front of the rim, then nudged the back. With just the right amount of touch on it, the ball fell in the basket.

"Yes!" I yelled. Angel and I rushed up to Rosie and gave her a high five.

"Thank you, Rosie!" Wil said, and she collapsed to the ground.

"Take a water break," Mr. Harris said, and both coaches laughed.

The coaches ran us through offenses and out-of-bounds plays. Then we split up into two teams

FRIDAY NIGHTS by Molly

and scrimmaged four-on-four. Anita, Jess, Penny, and I played against the others. Nobody officially kept score, but with Penny on my team, I knew we were winning. And that feeling was all I needed to keep me smiling as I raced up and down the floor. After about 10 minutes, the whistle blew and we merged at the center circle.

"Have a seat, girls," Mr. Harris said.

"We just wanted to tell you a little bit about the league," he continued. "It's the first time the city is doing this, so nothing is really set in stone. As far as we know, it's a league for girls going into sixth, seventh, and eighth grades. There are six teams. We play each team once and then there are two weeks of play-offs."

"From what we've heard, the other teams are pretty big and fast," my father said. "They have mostly eighth graders. We only have three, so it's not going to be easy."

"All we ask of you is to give it your best, no matter who you're up against," Mr. Harris added. "If we take it one game at a time, we've got nothing to worry about."

I eyed Mr. Harris suspiciously as my mind recalled the conversation I had overheard earlier. He was worried about something.

"We don't have the schedules yet," my dad added, "but this week's game is Friday at 7:00 right here. All games are on Fridays so you can play in your softball games on the weekends."

"Okay," Mr. Harris said, "on your feet!" We converged into a tight circle and piled our clammy hands in the center. After a count of three, we screamed, "Team!" The pack broke and we headed straight for the basketballs.

"Let's go now, girls," my dad called out firmly. "One more day of school and after that we can stay late and shoot."

"Why?" I whined. "We're not doing anything tomorrow."

"Let's go, Molls," he insisted.

As hard as it was to end our first night of practice together, we put the balls in the mesh bag and gathered our belongings. My dad threw the sack over his shoulder and the group began to filter out the door.

"Everybody ready?" I asked as I stood with my finger next to the light switch.

"Yeah," Penny said. "Hit it."

I killed the lights and dribbled through the darkness. One question kept running through my mind.

Who are the Hawks?

Chapter Three

On Wednesday, I walked down the aisle of the school bus, tossed my duffel bag down, and fell into the green seat. Penny pushed me over as she sat down next to me. Wil and Angel landed right ahead of us.

"It stinks that Rosie's not here," Penny said. "We should have snuck her on."

"Yeah, right," said Angel as she brushed her hair. "Everyone would have gone running to Mr. Gordon screaming about how a fifth grader was on the bus."

"When does Rosie find out about the all-star team?" Wil asked.

"This weekend," Penny replied.

"She better make it," I said.

"I'm tired of hearing people say whether or not a girl should be on the team," Wil said.

"It shouldn't even matter," Angel added.

"Everybody knows Rosie's good enough," Penny said.

I stared out the window not wanting to think about how unfair it would be for Rosie to not get what she deserved.

"How long of a drive is it?" Penny asked.

"About a half-hour," Wil replied.

I rolled up my towel in a ball, pressed it against the window, and rested my head on it. I shut out the noise, and stared blankly into the morning sun for a while. When we exited the highway, I spotted the Johnsville sign, and sat upright in my seat. All of our eyes drifted out the windows, and the chatter slowly faded.

"Are those houses or buildings?" Wil asked.

"That's going to be my house," J.J. boasted from the back seat as he pointed out the window to a huge colonial style home. A German shepherd darted out of the garage and wagged its tail on the front lawn. "But the dog's got to go," he added with a nervous laugh.

"If I had a house like that," Wil went on, "I'd charge people 50 cents—no, a dollar a tour."

"Check that one out," Penny said. "It looks like a hotel."

I stared into the houses looking for people, and began to wonder what life was like inside. I imagined having my very own bedroom where I could sleep without being kicked by my sister, and not having to fight over the bathroom. Then I pictured what I would see through my bedroom window if I lived in a place like Johnsville.

"If I had a house like that," I said pointing to a Victorian house with its own man-made pond, "I'd have a full-court in my backyard. Or a park. Yeah, a park. Anderson Park."

"Yeah," Wil agreed, and so did everyone else. "I'd have a pool too, though."

"Me too," Angel added.

"I could do without the pool," Penny said nervously, and we all laughed knowing Penny's fear of water. "If I had a big house like that—it would have to be in the city. The city is where I'm stayin'."

I sunk down in my seat. What Penny said made me realize how caught up I was in wanting something that wasn't mine. My brick house was simple and small. We had a small family room, a tiny kitchen and a master bedroom on the first floor. My sister and I slept in a canopy bed in one room upstairs, and my brothers slept in bunk beds next door to our room.

My father put an iron rim and a wooden backboard on a telephone pole in the backyard. We had just enough room to play. Out front, my mother dressed up the place by planting some flowers in the flowerpots that sat on our porch. And although the red station wagon in our slim driveway wasn't anything to brag about, our neighborhood was. If we needed anything, the Flanigans next door were always there for us. Even Old Man Miller, who walked his dog a dozen times a day and grumbled about all the noisy kids on the block, always made sure that we didn't walk home alone. Penny was right. We were city kids. And Broadway Avenue was ours.

The bus finally slowed down and turned into the circular driveway in front of Liberty Country Club. Yellow tulips covered a large portion of the perfectly manicured lawn. The shiny glass doors opened, and out came a man with a warm smile. It was Mr. Liberty. He extended his hand to Mr. Gordon, who was our principal at Lincoln. They chatted for a couple of quick seconds before Mr. Gordon stepped on our bus. Everyone looked up, and then slowly sank down in their seats. He began his speech about respecting the property, the people, each other, and being safe and smart in the pool.

"Mr. Liberty is a good friend of mine," Mr. Gordon's voice boomed, "and it's a privilege for us to be here. We're the only school he invites to visit. Now let's not ruin our privilege."

The bus was still. Even though we all thought Mr. Gordon was cool, no one ever dared to cross him. The second he stepped off the bus, everybody was up and rummaging around, reaching for snacks, coolers, towels and radios.

"Hey, Molly, I'll race you today?" Wil offered.

"Okay," I said. "Winner gets the extra cupcake."

"Your mom made those chocolate cupcakes with the vanilla frosting and rainbow sprinkles?" Wil asked excitedly.

I nodded proudly and she grinned.

"How 'bout Mike and I race you both?" Eddie asked, barging right into our conversation. I turned and glared at the biggest bully on Broadway.

"You couldn't beat us," I scoffed.

"Winners get two cupcakes," he offered.

"You brought cupcakes?" Wil asked surprisingly.

"Nope," Eddie said. "But we don't have to worry about it, because we're gonna win. What flavor did you say they were?"

I looked square in his dull eyes and slowly shook my head.

"If we win," Wil called out, "we get the bag of chips." Within an impressive few seconds, her eyes had scanned the boys' gear. She zeroed in on a bag of chips in the thin plastic grocery bag Mike was holding on his side.

"It's a deal," Eddie said sternly.

We streamed out of the buses and then through the front doors. Everyone rushed to beat the crowd through the locker room and out to the pool. Wil and Penny stopped to use the washroom while Angel and I hustled out onto the deck. We pulled three lawnchairs together and threw a bag on a fourth. Out of nowhere, Dawn walked up and grabbed two of our chairs.

"I'm saving these seats," Angel told Dawn with an incredible amount of composure.

Dawn, who was always starting some kind of trouble, looked around and then asked, "For who?"

"My friends," Angel said.

"Those sixth and seventh graders?" Dawn looked at me and laughed as she turned back to Angel. My blood boiled.

"Are you ever gonna grow up, Angel?" Dawn asked. "Or are you just gonna hang out with these chumps all your life?"

"You're the chump!" I shot back.

Angel kept her green eyes fixed on Dawn. "Molly, stay out of this," she said calmly. A few seconds passed, and Angel still wasn't moving.

"Whatever," Dawn mumbled. She let go of the chairs and strutted away. Without one single scoff or snicker, Angel simply reached up behind her head and tightened the bow in her hair. Then she picked up her towel and neatly laid it on her chair. I couldn't let what just happened pass so easily.

"Dawn's always starting trouble," I mumbled.

"She's not as tough as she acts," Angel said calmly. "She just puts on this front because she's afraid everybody will think she's soft. My mom tells me that some people are just like that. I guess they think they have to be that way."

I wondered what it was like to see everything through Angel's eyes. She never said any cuss words or called people bad names. Occasionally she would get mad at somebody during a game, and clock the person with one of her sharp elbows. But that was it.

It took me a while to understand why Angel was always so patient and understanding. I never knew until a couple months after she moved onto Broadway Ave. why she was nicknamed Angel and why her sister was named Faith. Some of our not-so-popular neighbors started spreading rumors that Angel's family were some kind of deeply religious Christians. They talked like we should be afraid of them. I didn't see what the big deal was. I was a Christian. A Catholic one. So after church one day, I asked my mother about Angel. She said that some people see themselves as being "saved." I thought I had been saved from lots of trouble many times in my life. So was I any different? I asked Penny once and she didn't know either. Nothing anyone said made any sense to me or to my friends. So we didn't even bother to waste any more time thinking about it.

"Angel!" Wil yelled, and they came running over. After dropping all of our belongings into a pile, we slipped off our shirts and shorts down to our bathing suits. I looked down at my pale Irish skin and folded my arms tightly in front of my chest. I thought about keeping my T-shirt on like Wil did.

"Molly, are you still breathing?" Penny quipped as she caught a flash of me. "You sure are pasty."

"You're almost see-through," Wil joked.

Everyone started laughing. I just rolled my eyes and tried to take it all in stride. It wasn't like I could defend myself. I was as white as they claimed. I slapped on some sunscreen, and threw the bottle at Penny when I was finished.

"Everybody ready?" Wil asked. We jumped up and race-walked across the deck.

"Slow down, ladies!" Mr. Gordon hollered.

We put on the brakes just before we walked down the stairs and into the water. Penny stopped in the shallow end. She never went into water over her waist. She always argued that it was physically impossible for her body to remain afloat. I had a hard time believing that an incredible athlete like Penny could not do such a simple thing.

"Come on out, P," I prodded, "you at least have to try."

"I'm trying," she shot back.

"Just a little further," I said.

"Are you crazy?" Penny hollered. She looked nothing like her usual cool self. "Go ahead without me."

"Stick your face in the water and blow some bubbles like this," I said. I giggled after I blew bubbles in the water.

"Really funny, Molly."

"Just try moving around a little bit where you are and then come out a little further," Wil said. "It's easy."

"No," Penny shot back sternly.

That was enough. Angel stayed to keep Penny company as Wil and I swam off. We both loved to swim underwater. I liked the peace and quiet, and especially the sensation of floating, which I never really could get on land.

"Don't look now," Wil said as she grabbed onto the side of the pool, "but trouble is slithering over."

"Hey, Molly, it looks like you've been working on your tan." Eddie grinned. I scowled at the creep.

"You ready to race?" Wil taunted. "I'm kind of hungry for some chips."

"You're always hungry," Eddie quipped.

"Shut up, jerk," I shot back.

Eddie ignored me. He turned and yelled at some kids to clear a lane across the pool. The traffic cleared, and slowly a crowd assembled against the wall. J.J. delegated himself as the judge. Eddie and I were up first, which left Wil against Mike for the finish.

"On your mark," J.J. bellowed. "Get set...Go!!"

I pushed off the wall and shot through the water. My arms flailed at first, and then I pulled myself forward. I kicked wildly while keeping an eye on Eddie underwater. On my last few strokes I took the lead, and then tagged the wall to release Wil. She started strong, but Mike caught up to her. They were even. Dead even. It was coming down to a perfectly timed last stroke. They both slapped the wall, and the crowd held its breath. Everyone looked up at J.J. who had laid out on his stomach and hung his head right over the wall. He raised his arm and pointed at Mike.

"No way, J!" I screamed. I shook my head as I glared at him.

He nodded his head and added with a smile, "Yes way, Molly!"

"That's not fair!" I yelled.

I looked at Eddie. He was grinning. "I prefer chocolate. Mike likes vanilla, but we're really not that picky."

I couldn't handle it. It just couldn't be. There was no way I could let Eddie beat me in front of dozens of kids and then sit there and rub my nose in it.

"Double or nothing," I shot back. "You win, you get four cupcakes. You lose, you owe us nothing."

Eddie scoffed arrogantly. "Don't start crying when you lose again."

"No, now wait a second, Molly. Come on," Wil begged me to think rationally as she gasped for air. "Do I get any say in this? Four cupcakes? Are you crazy? At least try and get some chips out of this."

"We can do it," I pleaded. But it wasn't enough. Whether we could do it was not the issue. Food was. "We win, and you get the extra cupcake and mine too. We lose, there's still one left for you. And my mom's got some extra at home."

Wil had no other choice but to support me. "All right," she said and she shrugged.

"I'm going last this time," I said. Now I just needed to buy some recovery time for Wil.

"We can't start without J.J.," I said. Everyone looked around.

"Where's J?" Mike asked.

"He's coming," Angel yelled.

"Stalling isn't gonna do you any good," Eddie said.

I ignored him and turned to Wil. "You start this time," I said. I wanted to be the one to finish the race. "You can do it. Just stay with him. And I'll bring us in."

I looked up and saw J.J. flexing his muscles in front of a group of girls on the deck.

"Yo, J!" Eddie called out. "You done?"

"The girls are loving this," J.J. added proudly as the crowd laughed. He turned and flexed for all the people in the pool.

"Let the games begin," J.J. bellowed. "Everybody ready?"

"Yeah," I said. "We've been waiting for you."

J.J. pretended to hold a starter's pistol in his hand. "Swimmers take your mark, get set, go!"

Mike quickly built a three-stroke lead and held it the whole way. My heart began to race. I took one deep breath as I waited patiently for Wil to touch. I pushed off the wall and ripped through the water. I peeked up once and saw Eddie's feet. *Catch him, Molly. Catch him!* I swam so hard that the muscles in my arms began to burn. I hit the wall and pushed off. When I turned to the side, I saw Eddie's whole body. I had moved in right next to him with half-a-lap remaining. I pulled hard on my last two strokes, stretched out, slapped the wall, and whipped my head out of the water. J.J. was pointing at me, and Wil was screaming like crazy. Mr. Gordon, who had bent down next to him, confirmed the decision.

"Molly by about that much," Mr. Gordon said, and he held his hands about four inches apart.

I struggled to breathe, even though I didn't really need air. I felt thoroughly invigorated. "We did it, Wil!" I gasped.

"You did it, Molly," Wil said. "Way to go. Now let's go eat. All this swimming has made me hungry."

I laughed as I followed Wil's lead. We pulled ourselves up the ladder and out of the pool. I looked down and grinned smugly at Eddie, who was still holding onto the side.

"They're chocolate," I said. Eddie swiped the surface of the water with the palm of his hand. His splash barely reached me.

"I'll give you a head start next time, Eddie," I said as I walked away.

Penny and Angel, who had stood poolside and rooted wildly for us the whole way, had the snacks and drinks already out. I collapsed on the lawn chair.

"The things you will do for a lousy cupcake," Penny said and we all laughed.

"Wil," Angel asked. "How are you gonna eat two cupcakes at 10:00 in the morning?"

"Watch me," Wil said.

"You'll be sick," she said.

"No I won't," Wil shot back.

"I got some apples and oranges," I offered.

"Eat some of them," Angel said to Wil.

"Fine," Wil said. "But I still get my cupcakes."

There was no arguing with her, so Angel and I dropped it. J.J. came over and sat down on the end of one of the lawn chairs.

"Did you come to mooch some food off of us, J.J., or what?" Wil asked.

"Nice of you to offer," J.J. said. "I just wanted to tell you that I heard you were in a league this summer on Friday nights. I was at my cousin Tasha's house this weekend, and she said she's playing, too."

"What grade is she going into?" Penny asked.

"Eighth," J.J. said.

"Is she any good?" Angel asked.

"Yeah, of course she can play. She's *my* cousin," he added pointing to himself.

"Then we've got nothing to be worried about," Penny joked, and she tossed a can of soda to him.

"Tasha's real strong," he added, "and some of her friends are really tall."

"Everybody's tall to you," quipped Wil.

"Ha, ha," J.J. said, "and everybody is skinny to you."

"Oh, cut it out," Penny stepped in as usual. "Please, don't start."

"Whatever," J.J. mumbled. "All you need to know is Tasha can *play*."

"Whose team is she on?" I asked.

"I don't know," he replied. "She lives over on the East Side, so whatever team that is."

"Are they any good?"

"She says they're stacked with the best players in the city," he said.

"We'll see about that," Wil muttered, and she licked the frosting off of her second cupcake.

Chapter Four

"**M**olly!" my older brother Kevin yelled from the kitchen. "Are you gonna help?"

I exaggerated a groan, and didn't budge from the couch. It had been a long afternoon at the pool. My sun-burned body sizzled and my bloodshot eyes burned.

"Come on, Molly," he continued, "before Dad gets home."

"Is it ready?" I slurred loudly with my face buried in a cushion.

"Yeah," he replied. "Ma just called and told me to take the pork chops and potatoes out."

Our mother worked evenings as a nurse at the city hospital. Like most nights, she had left prepared dinners in the oven and the directions on the kitchen table.

"Would you come on?" Kevin pleaded.

He was really getting on my nerves. "Would you be quiet!" I screamed back. I pulled myself up off the couch and dragged myself into the kitchen. Annie and I finished setting the table just as Dad walked in the door.

"Hi kids," he said and smiled. He put his arm around Frankie and gave him a hug.

"Can we go to practice tonight, Dad?" Frankie asked.

"Only if you're good," he replied.

"Yes!" Annie exclaimed.

Frankie and Annie scurried around in the kitchen, and then landed in their seats. Kevin kept a close eye on them as he poured the milk. One false move by anyone and he would be stuck home baby-sitting.

Frankie lazily reached across the table for his glass. He stuck one finger out and pulled it toward him. It tipped. He reached for it but it was too late. When the milk spilled all over the table, Kevin's eyes bulged.

"Uh-oh," Annie said softly. I put my index finger over my lips and glared at her. Kevin swiped a towel off the stove and quietly raced back to the table. All eyes turned to our father. His back was to us. He was washing his hands. The noise from the running tap water was all he had heard. I glanced back at Kevin. His angry eyes suddenly begged me for help. I hurried to the kitchen sink.

"So Dad," I said. "You hear anything else about the league?"

"No," he said. He finished lathering the soap in his hands.

"Are there any really good teams?"

"I'm not sure." He put his hands under the faucet.

"Do you think we can win it?" I asked.

He rinsed his right hand and then his left. "I don't know. We haven't even played one game yet,

Molly. You shouldn't even be talking about winning it."

He tightened the knob and the water stopped. When he reached for a paper towel, my eyes shifted nervously to Kevin. He gave me the nod. The mess on the kitchen table had disappeared. I breathed a deep sigh of relief.

After a peaceful dinner and an efficient clean-up, we had passed the test. Frankie and Annie raced out the door and into the car. I threw the bag of basketballs over my shoulder and walked down the steps. We piled in and waited for our father.

"Who needs a ride?" he asked when he sat down in the front seat.

"Anita and Mary," I said.

We drove down Broadway and stopped to pick them up.

"Hi, girls," my dad said.

"Hi, Mr. O," Mary replied.

"Jess said she couldn't come," Anita added after she shut the door.

"Why?" my father asked.

Anita shrugged. My father just shook his head. "At first, I was afraid we would have too many girls interested. Now we barely have enough."

"And Jen is out of town," Mary added.

"Is anyone else not going to be able to make it?" he asked. This time Mary shrugged. "How are we going to be able to play if we can't even get everyone at practice?"

Nobody answered. Some of the kids on Broadway Ave. had things going on in their lives that the rest of us didn't know much about—family problems and other private matters. Penny and I were the lucky ones as far as I could see. Our parents were still together, and aside from some arguments, mostly about us, they seemed happy.

I didn't know much about Rosie's home life. It was hard to tell because her father could be so tough on her during games and practices. And all I knew about Mrs. Jones was that she was a sweet lady who could really cook.

Our not-so-popular neighbors said that Angel's parents were having problems. Angel didn't say anything about it, and we didn't ask.

The only way I found out about Wil was through Penny. And Penny really didn't know that much either. Wil's mother had died when she was nine years old. I remember holding my mother's hand at the funeral as I watched my friend sit next to her father in the front row. Wil's face was dry, and she looked right past Penny and me when we walked by. She was still in shock. Seeing her like that left me asking questions for a long time. But in about a week or so after the burial, Wil was back at the park playing ball and gabbing away as if nothing happened. My mother said it would be all right if we tried to get her to talk about it. We tried, but Wil never said a word.

While none of our families really had much money, Wil's family had it the hardest. A couple years after Wil's mother had died, Mr. Thomas re-married a woman with three young boys. Wil and her little sister, Louise, made room in their small apartment for everyone else.

As for Jess, Mary, Jen, and Anita, they had their share of problems, too. My father did his best to try and help all the girls in any way he could. Sometimes I asked what was going on. He always said that if it didn't concern me, I didn't have a right to know. I hated this answer because it sounded like he was calling me nosy, and I wasn't nosy. I was just concerned. I wanted to help because we were all friends. My dad told me that the best way I could help was by doing just that. By being a friend.

My father parked the car and we all piled out. Kevin unlocked the door. I ran to the lights and flicked the switch. Just as the gym began to brighten, Frankie stole a ball away from Annie.

"I'm telling Dad," Annie whined.

"Don't be such a baby," I said.

"I'm not a baby," she shot back.

"Then go get it back from him," I said.

She took off. I pulled another ball out of the bag. A stinging chill from my sunburn ran down my back as I started to dribble around. Rosie ran into the gym and waved. Then she picked up a ball and started practicing her full-court lay-ups. If only she could have passed some of her energy around to the rest of us. Angel sat down on the floor and didn't move for five minutes except to brush her hair. Penny kept yawning. Wil walked into the gym without her usual goofy smile. She removed her glasses and rubbed her sleepy eyes.

"I just woke up," she mumbled as she put her glasses back on. Then she slicked back her hair and tied it into a bun. I went over and dragged Angel off of the ground as everyone else arrived.

All it took were a few competitive games to wipe away our sluggishness. After about 10 minutes, my dad blew his whistle and we jogged to center court.

"Who are we playing on Friday, Mr. O?" Rosie asked.

"The Rockford Rockets," my dad replied.

"Are they any good?" asked Wil.

"If we play the way we're capable of, we can play with anyone," he said.

"Yeah, I know," mumbled Wil, who didn't take his response as a straight answer. "But can we beat them?"

"Sure we can," Mr. Harris said. "It's going to take a big effort by everyone."

I don't know why Wil insisted on getting any inside information. She knew the scoop on Rockford. We all did.

"Girls, we just wanted to talk you through a couple things on defense," Mr. Harris said. "The best player for Rockford is a stocky power forward."

"Sheila?" Angel gasped. It all came back to her like a bad dream. But it wasn't a dream. It was a flashback of something real.

Penny and I went to watch Angel play against Sheila's team in a softball game at Rockford Park a year ago in June. With the score tied in the bottom of the seventh, a batter nailed a shot into the outfield and Angel made a dash for home plate. Just as she rounded third base, everyone in the ballpark gasped in fear. The center fielder's throw was right on. And Sheila, the catcher, who had planted her thick body on home plate, grinned devilishly with ball in hand. Penny and I screamed "Stop!" But Angel had her mind made up. Her courageous attempt to slide turned into a ugly spill with legs and arms flying all over the place. Although no bones were broken, Angel was shaken up for a couple of days. She always claimed that her body had never fully recovered.

"Oh no," Angel mumbled. "Not Sheila."

At five-feet 10-inches, and an unknown official weight, we considered Sheila a team wrecking ball. She plowed people over on her way to the basket.

"Wil," Mr. Harris said seriously, "she's your assignment for the game."

I turned to Wil expecting sheer panic. When a smile crept onto her face, I shook my head in amazement. Of all things to do in this potentially disastrous situation, Wil was blushing. She was simply bursting with pride. Guarding Sheila was no small task. But to Wil, the ultimate team player, it meant everything.

The strategy was simple. All the other players on the floor, except Anita, would have to help Wil by doing all they could to prevent Sheila from touching the ball. It only made sense to keep Anita, our scoring center, as far away from Sheila as possible.

"Everyone understand?" my dad asked, and we all nodded our heads.

The coaches divided us into four-on-four teams. Kevin jumped down from the stage to be the eighth player. In the middle of our scrimmage, some boys walked into the gym. I only recognized Mike, Marvin, and Beef. Beef, who just finished the seventh grade, was short for Beef Potato. We never knew his real name. The rumor was that his older brother named him Beef for his hearty appetite. Then somebody made up the last name of Potato, and it stuck. After a while, everybody had so much fun calling him Beef Potato, we didn't care what his real name was. And neither did he.

The boys squirmed around in the bleachers. After about five minutes, they lost all patience. The open basket in front of them was too enticing. One by one they crept onto the floor and started shooting.

"Hold it!" my dad yelled. "This isn't open gym. What are you guys doing here?"

"We've got practice," Beef said.

"At what time?" my dad asked.

"Eight-thirty."

"Who's your coach?"

The gym door opened. Beef pointed to the man standing in the doorway.

"What's the problem?" the man asked.

"We've got the gym until nine," my dad said.

"I didn't think the girls would..." the man began.

His voice trailed off. There was no need to finish. We knew what he was going to say. The surprised look on his face was because we—the girls—were still in the gym playing hard and serious basketball.

I clicked my tongue, Wil rolled her eyes, and Angel scoffed.

"Here we go again," mumbled Penny.

I turned to my father. His face was scarlet. Mr. Harris calmly grabbed his arm, and whispered something. My father took a deep breath and regained his composure.

"Let's work something out," Mr. Harris said.

My jaw dropped. *Are you crazy? Kick 'em out!*

"If the boys are here early, that's fine with us," Mr. Harris went on. "But they have to scrimmage against us to stay."

"Who says we wanna play them?" I shouted.

The man raised his eyebrow at me.

Mr. Harris ignored me so I turned to my father. His eyes told me to relax. *Why?* I glanced around looking for a logical explanation. When I counted our seven players, I figured it out. We needed bodies.

I glanced back to the boys' coach. He paused, almost as if he was not sure if Mr. Harris was serious, and then turned to his team. "It's up to you guys."

Some boys half-smiled, and others just shrugged. Beef finally spoke up. "We'll play," he said surely, as if the others were crazy to even think of refusing.

"Get five together, and we'll bring the ball down in a second," Mr. Harris said. He hustled across half court to our end of the floor.

"All right," Mr. Harris called out enthusiastically. Then he looked over his shoulder at the boys shooting at the other end. "Wil, Penny, Molly, Anita and Rosie: you're in. We're going to play Beef as if he were Sheila."

All eyes turned to Beef. I imagined him with a wig on. Penny must have too. She chuckled, and then Angel burst out laughing.

"They do kind of look alike," Angel joked as we threw our hands in the huddle.

"Let's show 'em now," Mr. Harris said seriously, and the laughter subsided. The determined look on his face said it all. It was more than just a scrimmage.

At each position, we were overmatched by both skill and athleticism, except for Penny. She could do anything she wanted. The rest of us ran around aimlessly. It seemed every move, every pass, every shot was such an effort. The boys took advantage of every mistake. After they ran off a series of steals and easy baskets, we started bickering.

"Get open," I said.

"I am," Wil shot back. "Try making a good pass."

"Who's got him?" Angel snapped after Mike scored again.

"I don't!" Anita shot back.

"Time out!" my dad hollered.

We jogged shamefully over to the side.

"Girls, settle down," he said. "You're putting too much pressure on yourselves. Relax. Rely on each other a bit more."

"Don't stand still. You're standing too close together. Spread out," Mr. Harris reeled off. "Move without the ball. And make good passes."

"You're a much better team then they are," my dad added. I gazed past our huddle, and saw the boys laughing and joking at the other end of the floor. Frustration spread through me. I turned to Penny and could see the daggers in her eyes.

"Let's play," she said firmly and she reached out and slapped my hand. We marched back onto the court and called out our match-ups. Penny picked off a steal and scored a lay-up at the other end. Wil pulled down a rebound over Beef, and I hit a jumpshot on our next possession. We smoothly and confidently popped the ball around on offense. And on defense, we double-teamed Beef, just as we had planned against Sheila.

"Help out on Sheila," I yelled once by mistake. "Oops. I mean Beef."

When Penny made the same name mistake, Beef bricked a lay-up and then fumbled a pass.

"Come on, Beef!" he yelled to himself.

Mr. Harris blew the whistle.

"That's it," he called out. "Nice job kids."

Although there was no official score, I knew that we had lost. I walked off to the water fountain, unable to look my teammates in the eye.

Mr. Harris thanked the boys for scrimmaging against us. "You're welcome here every night at 8:30 if you agree to play like you did tonight," he offered. "What do ya say, guys?" he asked.

All the boys nodded their heads in agreement. It struck me then that maybe the only point that mattered in the last half-hour was the one we proved.

"O.K., Mr. H," Beef lamented, "but no more calling me Sheila." Mr. Harris laughed, and I apologized to Beef.

The boys' coach approached my father and Mr. Harris at center circle. "Those girls aren't that bad," he said.

My dad looked him right in the eyes said, "You mean, those players aren't that bad."

A chill shot up my spine. That said it all. We walked off the floor and left the speechless man behind.

Chapter Five

The moment I walked into the gym, I stopped dead in my tracks. My eyes locked on the ominous figure standing at the other end of the floor. Sheila's messy hair was tied in a bundle on the top of her head. She scowled as she pounded the ball on the hardwood. Then she reached her heavy arms up, banged the ball off the backboard and ripped it down.

"She looks like a giant," I whispered to Penny.

"Quit staring, Molly," she replied.

"I'm not," I said.

"You were," Penny said.

Penny was pretty good at making me feel awful sometimes. I dropped my head in shame. My stocky body wasn't much to brag about. I thought about how my uncles and bullies like Eddie called my brother Frankie and me things like "Porky" and "Egghead." I couldn't imagine all the awful things other kids called Sheila.

We set our gym bags on our bench and began to warm-up at our end. Wil's nerves had already taken control of her. She twisted her hands in her shirt and then started tugging on her shorts. Almost every time a pass was thrown to her, she fumbled it. Then she started joking around.

"Shoot a three, P!" she cheered.

"Let's go, Wil," Mr. Harris said. "Get your head into the game." Wil's smiling lips fell into a straight line.

When we walked out to the center circle for tip-off, butterflies fluttered in my stomach. The second the ball went up, all the anxiety disappeared.

"Let's go, Blue!" my dad cheered.

The game started with both teams matching baskets. Then Sheila moved Wil out of the way for an offensive rebound, and two points.

"Wil, don't let her get going!" Penny ordered. Wil nodded, and her worried face grew intense.

We pulled ahead by 10 points at the end of the half. When the third quarter began, Penny continued with her ball-handling show. Rosie picked off three passes, while Anita grabbed every other rebound. Then there was me. I was terrible. No, I was awful. It was one of those days where I just couldn't get out of my own way.

"Bull," Mr. Harris yelled to me, "slow down!"

He nicknamed me "Bull" one day at the park when I went out of control, hustling all over the place. I didn't know what he meant by it. So I asked him. He told me that I was like a bull in a china shop crashing down everything and anything in my path.

"Just relax," he said later as I walked out of our huddle. But slowing down never seemed to work. With every mistake I made, I kept pressing harder. I just threw myself all over the floor, hoping something good would come of it. Nothing did.

At the end of the third quarter, I turned to Wil. Her black hair had fallen out of her rubber band. She stood drenched in sweat.

"Good job, Wil," I whispered as the coaches spoke.

She had held Sheila to 10 points and helped draw four fouls against her. One more foul and Sheila would be out of the game.

"Last quarter, Wil, and it's all over," Angel said as we broke from the huddle. Wil raised her eyebrows and dramatically took in a deep breath.

"I don't know if I can make it," she grumbled.

The ball went down on the block to Sheila three times in a row, and she scored on each opportunity. Wil caught my bounce pass on the other end, and courageously took it right back at her. Sheila reached up, swatted the shot out of bounds, and knocked Wil to the floor.

No foul was called. "What was that?" I threw my arms up in the air and scowled at the referee. He ignored me as he retrieved the ball, which made me irate. I rushed to pick up Wil, who had been lying on the court motionless.

"You alright?" I asked.

"Yeah," Wil whimpered as she grabbed her side.

"Give me the ball next time down, will ya, P?" I asked.

Penny looked at me and took a deep breath. "Fine, but don't go doin' anything stupid."

My best friend passed me the ball on our next possession. I dropped my head and fiercely drove down the lane. Even when Sheila moved fully into my view, I refused to let up. I barreled forward and jumped up. I quickly recognized the danger right before my eyes, so I picked my knees up to protect myself. I walloped Sheila solidly in the chest and we both went crashing to the floor. When the whistle shrieked, I didn't bother looking at the referee. I knew I had just completed my best imitation of a bull in a china shop. I gladly accepted my offensive foul.

"You're crazy, Molly!" Penny muttered as her wide eyes watched Sheila slowly rise. "She's gonna get you for that one."

I shrugged. "What's she gonna do?"

Penny didn't answer. She didn't have to. I watched Sheila stare blankly ahead. Her lips were pursed. Her fists were clenched. Without one word, she marched down the floor and took over the game. She scored two baskets with players hanging on her.

"Would somebody help me, please?" Wil yelled.

"I'm trying," Anita said.

"Well try harder!"

All of us tried to help Wil. But it didn't matter. Sheila continued to score. I looked up at the clock. With two minutes left, the score was tied. Penny passed the ball into Wil. She gathered what little energy she had stored, leaned into Sheila, and threw up a prayer. The whistle shrieked, and the referee threw one arm up in the air and pointed the other at Sheila.

"Yes!" I cheered.

It was Sheila's fifth foul. Twenty-two points later, the scoring machine was finally out of the game for good. We all collapsed on Wil, in a high-fiving celebration.

The Rockets could not do much without Sheila. We went on to win by three points. When the final buzzer sounded, I gave Wil another hard, stinging high-five.

"Ow," she said as she shook her hand.

"Way to go, Wil!" I yelled and everyone huddled around her again. We appreciated Wil's big-boned body like never before. She was too exhausted to speak.

We broke out of our circle to slap hands with the Rockets. I started through the line thinking only of Sheila. My knee-first tackle had to hurt. *What would she say? What would she do?* I felt her moving closer. I picked my head up and looked her square in the eyes.

"Good game," she said, and she kept walking.

My mouth dropped open. *Why didn't she care?* I was still in shock when I heard my dad yell, "Ballplayers, over here!"

I jogged over in a daze.

"Nice job tonight," my father said. "Who wants pizza?"

We all cheered.

"Take a schedule before you go," Mr. Harris said and he passed out the copies.

I picked up a schedule and glanced down the list of teams. My eyes stopped and stared at the name, The East Side Hawks. I matched up our numbers, and saw that we were playing in one week.

"Yes!" I said aloud.

"What are you so excited about?" Penny asked.

"Nothing," I mumbled. "I just can't wait to play again. That's all."

I decided to keep the information I had gathered from the coaches to myself. There was no need to alarm anyone else. And I couldn't bare to give

J.J. the satisfaction of thinking that we might be worried about playing against anyone, especially his cousin.

Later that night while we were devouring two jumbo pizzas, Penny and Wil re-enacted me tackling Sheila. My friends found it all very entertaining. I didn't see why it was so funny.

"You should be a stunt-woman," Wil said.

"It wasn't that bad," I muttered and then I turned to Rosie for support. She wouldn't say anything. "Was it that bad?"

"Yeah it was," she said softly. Everyone started laughing again. My face burned in embarrassment.

Later that night, my father drove down Broadway Ave. and dropped my friends off at their homes. After he parked the car, I slowly stepped out and dragged my tired body up our driveway. A voice called through the darkness.

"Hey, Molly. Did you win?"

It was J.J. I turned and spotted his silhouette in his bedroom window.

"Yeah, we won."

"How many did you score?"

"Not many at all," I said lowly. I hated when people asked that question, even after games when I did score a lot. It was a team game. Wins and losses were all that mattered to me.

"My auntie just called," he said. "Tasha's team won by 42 points."

Forty-two points! My eyes almost popped out of my head. But J.J. couldn't see me in the dark.

"She says her team is going to kick everybody's butt, including yours next Friday night," he added.

"Shut up, J," I grumbled.

"For real," he said raising his tone.

"Yeah, whatever, J," I called out. "I'll see you tomorrow at the park, and I'll kick your butt."

J.J. blurted out some more nonsense. I just laughed obnoxiously over his voice as I jogged into my house.

Chapter Six

With one out left, I kicked the dirt around first base, and then crouched into my ready position.

"One to go," Penny yelled from shortstop.

"Play's at first," said Wil, who was catching behind the plate. Angel cocked back her arm, and then let the ball fly right down the pipe. The ball jumped off the bat and headed between second and third base.

"It's over," Wil called out.

With Rosie at short, and Penny at third, nothing got by. Rosie took two quick sidesteps, and eyed the ball into her glove. I set my foot on first base and waited. She smoothly fired the perfect throw right into my mitt.

"Way to play, Rosie!" I screamed as we all jogged in. The game had ended, and so did our morning of park-district softball. We had won both games easily.

"It's hot!" Angel said. "Let's go get some freeze pops."

We raced over to the concession stand.

"Anyone have to use the bathroom?" I asked along the way.

"Yeah," Rosie said, "I do."

I led the way through the crowd, and Rosie followed behind me. We walked inside the small restroom and waited in a short line. Rosie went in right before me. Then my turn came. I hurried in.

"Molly," I heard Rosie's voice call. "You still in here?"

"Yeah," I said. I found it strange that Rosie was so concerned.

"I..I..was just wondering," Rosie added nervously.

I unhooked the latch, pushed open the door, then froze. My biggest nightmare stood right before my eyes. It was Sheila.

"Say, Red, you were on the team we played against last night," she said, calling me by the color of my hair. Her voice left me dumbfounded. Sheila sounded as if she had just sucked on a helium balloon.

"You played at Lincoln last night, didn't you?" she squeaked.

I nodded my head nervously. I took one look into Rosie's wide eyes. I wanted to tell her to make a run for it before Sheila noticed we were together. But Rosie didn't move. Suddenly my knees felt weak and my eyes shifted around the room to locate all possible exits. My life was going to end in a smelly public bathroom.

"You all are pretty good," Sheila added.

My jaw dropped. "Thanks," I muttered.

"What's your name, Red?"

"Molly."

"I'm Sheila," she squeaked.

I looked down to the ground in utter shame for all the awful things I thought about Sheila.

"You all right?" she asked.

"I'm sorry about running into you like I did last night," I mumbled. I couldn't pick my head up as I spoke. "I shouldn't have done that to you."

"That's O.K.," Sheila said. "I'm kinda used to it. I'll forgive you," she then paused and grinned. "Well, this time, anyway."

"This is my friend, Rosie," I said. Rosie looked straight up at Sheila.

"Does she talk?" Sheila asked.

"She's shy," I explained. "She played last night."

"Yeah, I know." Sheila said. "When do you play against the Hawks?"

"This Friday night," I said.

"They're *good,* " she added. "I heard they won by 42 points last night."

"I know," I mumbled.

The more we talked, the more I relaxed. Sheila no longer looked anything like the freak my mind created her to be.

"I really gotta go, Red," Sheila said in a hurry. It was her turn in line. She winced as she walked toward the stall. "Maybe I'll see you two in the play-offs. Good luck against the Hawks."

"Bye, Sheila," I said.

Rosie and I sprinted out the door to catch up with the rest of the group.

"You are not going to believe this!" I exclaimed.

"What?" Penny asked.

"You are not going to believe who we just saw in the bathroom."

"Who?" Wil begged.

"Hey you, Ballplayers," a voice shouted. "You really think you can play?"

I turned around and saw four angry girls heading toward us.

"We heard that you've been talking about winning the league this summer," a muscular girl said as she glared at Penny. "And we've got something to say about it."

Then she turned to me. I took one look at her almond eyes and gap-toothed smile. She looked just like J.J. It had to be Tasha. She had the rest of the Hawks at her side. The only one I recognized was Betsy Miner. She used to live three blocks south of the park before she moved to the East Side. Now she was a Hawk, too.

"How could we say anything?" Penny said trying to ease the situation. "We don't even know you."

"Who are you, anyway?" Angel snapped.

"We're the Hawks," Tasha said. "The East Side Hawks. And you'll get to know us real well after we teach you a lesson next Friday night."

"Yeah, right," I mumbled as I rolled my eyes.

"You got something to say?" Betsy shot back at me.

I scoffed arrogantly.

"How about we teach you your first lesson right now?" Tasha asked.

She reached out and shoved Penny, but Penny didn't move. Tasha shoved her again. And that was it. I had seen enough. I got a running start and jumped on Tasha's back. She reached behind me and grabbed my ponytail. Betsy darted after Wil.

"Penny!" Wil screamed. Penny and Angel jumped forward and threw their arms around Betsy. I let go of Tasha's back and stumbled to the ground. I caught my balance, swung and missed. Rosie got a running start and tried to tackle Tasha. Skinny little Rosie must not have realized that Tasha was twice her body weight. Tasha pushed Rosie away, curled her fist and nailed me in the stomach. I grabbed her waist and pulled her down to the ground. She quickly flipped on top of me and pinned me to the dirt. I squirmed and grunted, but it didn't do any good. I watched her silhouette wind up.

"Oh no!" Rosie yelled.

"Don't!" Penny screamed.

Out of nowhere, I watched a large hand grab Tasha's fist, and a forearm slung around her neck. Tasha released me. I sat up and squinted through the sunlight. Sheila was holding Tasha in a head-lock. The rest of the Hawks stood motionless as Tasha flopped around like a fish out of water.

"Why you gotta be so mean?" Sheila squeaked.

"Lemme go!" Tasha yelled.

Sheila gently released her. Tasha brushed off the dirt on her shirt and slicked back her hair.

"We'll see you again real soon," she muttered. Then she and the Hawks turned and walked away.

"Thanks, Sheila," I said as I rose from the ground.

"No problem," she said. "I don't like those Hawks much anyway."

I looked to my friends whose eyes were bulging.

"This is Sheila," I said. "We met Sheila in the bathroom."

Sheila glanced around and smiled sheepishly. When no one moved, I nudged Penny with my elbow.

"Hey," Penny finally said, and she extended her hand to slap her five. "Thanks for pulling Molly out of that mess."

Then my best friend turned to me. "You're lucky. If it weren't for Sheila..."

"You want a freeze pop?" Rosie asked.

"Sure," Sheila said. Rosie bent over to pick up the unopened freeze pops that Wil had dropped on the ground. She wiped them on her shirt and handed a purple one to Sheila.

"Now that we're friends, Sheila, you got to promise you'll take it easy next time on us," Angel joked. "Keep it below 10 points."

Sheila laughed.

"You're really good, Sheila," Wil said.

"Thanks. So are you. Heck, you beat us."

"You should come play at the park with us some-time," Penny said.

"What park?"

"Anderson Park. It's our park. Right off Broad-way."

"Give me a call, and I'll take the bus up some-time," she said. Sheila politely asked for a pencil from one of the mothers at the concession stand. She scribbled down her phone number on a nap-kin and handed it to Penny.

"I gotta go," she said and she headed off. I yelled good-bye as I watched her jog through the parking lot.

● ● ● ●

Later that night, I told my father that I met Sheila.

"She's really nice, Dad," I said. I quickly made the decision to leave out the minor details of her saving my life.

"I'm sure she is," he said. "Just because she's bigger than everyone else, doesn't mean she's any different."

"I know," I said. "We saw the team we're playing Friday night, too."

"Oh," he said. "The Hawks?" He waited for me to go on.

"They're pretty big," I said.

I left it at that. If I had told the fighting part of the story, I wouldn't have seen the light of day for a long time. It didn't make any sense to subject myself to such punishment, especially in the summertime. So I let it slide.

I just crossed my fingers behind my back and hoped he wouldn't find out from anyone else.

Chapter Seven

I grabbed my radio and set it down on the back porch. I had made a habit out of shooting alone in the backyard at least once a day. It helped me sort out the heavy thoughts that weighed down my mind. And the Hawks had been in my head all week.

After a couple minutes, I felt the eyes of another person staring at me. Without looking, I knew exactly who it was. I had told Billy Flanigan at least a million times to just come outside and shoot with me when he saw me at the basket. But he always needed a personal invitation.

He started his routine. It began at his back window where he stared outside for about five minutes. I looked up to him occasionally, but he would always turn away. So I just dribbled and shot some more. Just when I thought he had given up, I would hear his back door slam. Then I would hear his ball bounce. He would stay at the same spot on the sidewalk dribbling for another five minutes. It was at this point where I lost all patience.

"Billy, you wanna come over and shoot?" I asked.

As I predicted, he shrugged his shoulders. I took a couple more shots, hoping Billy would stop being so stubborn. But he never gave in on the first try.

"Bill, come on over," I commanded.

And that did it. He skipped over, unlatched the gate, and dribbled on what had to be one of his favorite places on earth.

Billy Flanigan's all-time favorite place to be was a toss up between the fire department where his father worked or at the actual scene of any fires in the city. At the age of 12, Billy was already a legend on Broadway Ave. for his fascination with fires. Whenever he heard the local fire department siren sound off, he dropped everything, sprinted into his house, and put his ear to his father's scanner. If the fire was close enough, he jumped on the banana seat of his bicycle and pedal frantically to the site of the commotion. It didn't matter if it was a blaze or a mere false alarm.

"Any fires in the past couple days, Billy?" I asked.

"One grass fire in a field on the West Side on Monday afternoon around 4:30. And somebody lit up a garbage dumpster early Tuesday morning. Around 3:00. A little shed caught on fire. It was by some of the apartments by Lincoln."

"Really? I didn't hear about that. Was anybody hurt?"

"No," he mumbled. "It was just some stupid kids causing trouble. They're lucky though."

Kids in the neighborhood made up jokes about Billy and his passion for firefighting. They picked on Billy and his younger brother Bobby for other reasons, too. The Flanigan boys went to a special education school instead of Lincoln. When other kids like Eddie teased Billy and Bobby, it really set me off. The Flanigans were the kind of people who would give you the shirt off their backs, and any food they had in the refrigerator. So as stubborn as Billy Flanigan was when it came to shooting baskets, I tried not to get too upset with him.

"We're playing the Hawks tonight," I told him. "I can't stand them. You wanna come watch the game?"

"Yeah, if my mom lets me," he said as he sunk his favorite shot from deep in the left-hand corner.

"Watch this!" Frankie screamed. Billy and I turned and watched my younger brother hold his hands up in the air as he zoomed down the alley on his bicycle. "No hands!"

"Slow down, Frank!" I yelled. Even at a moderate speed, he was a shaky driver. Watching him made me nervous. He hit a bump and the handlebars wobbled.

"Look out!" I screamed.

His bike jack-knifed and he went flying head first into the aluminum garbage cans. Billy sprinted over to Frankie first. Then I jogged over, keeping my cool, just as my mother had taught us.

"Are you all right, Frank?" I asked.

He screamed and carried on.

"Settle down," I said. "You're OK."

When he turned over, blood gushed from his chin.

"Oh, no!" Billy shrieked.

Frankie started hyperventilating.

"Take it easy," I said. "It's not that bad."

He finally calmed down, and we walked him into the house.

"What's the matter?" Annie asked. Her eyes widened when she saw the blood. "Is Frankie okay?"

"He's fine," I said. "It's just a little cut."

"Are you gonna call mom?" she asked.

I nodded. Kevin had already left for his baseball game, which left me in charge. I remained calm, but poor Billy was still all shook up.

"Billy, would you grab me some ice out of the fridge and put it in a paper towel?"

He jumped up, ran to the refrigerator, ripped out the ice cube tray, and dropped it on the floor.

"Sorry," he said as he scooped up the ice cubes. Annie bent over to help him.

I picked up the phone with my free hand and called my mother at work. She told me to wait until Dad came home. He walked in the door 15 minutes later.

"Easy, Frank," my dad said as my brother whimpered. He gently picked up Frankie's chin.

"Looks like we're going to be visiting mom at the hospital tonight," he said.

Frankie gasped.

"Molly," my dad said, "call Mr. Harris and ask for a ride to the game."

"You can't come, Dad?" I whined. I needed him there.

"I can't leave Frankie like this," he said.

I huffed as I walked over to the phone. Mrs. Harris answered and she said it was okay when I asked if Billy could come, too. I made two peanut butter sandwiches and we ate them as we walked down to Penny's.

"You ready to play, Molly?" Penny asked me as she skipped down her steps. It seemed that the Hawks even got under Penny's skin after the stunt they pulled at the softball tournament.

"Yep," I said.

I walked into the gym that night and the first person I saw was Tasha. She was looking at me, too. I didn't want to be the first to turn away, so I kept glaring at her. Finally, she turned and shot her ball at the basket.

Just before game time, Mr. Harris brought us together in a tight huddle. He tried to give us all he could on how to play against the Hawks.

"You gotta move the ball on offense. Don't get caught in their traps. Make sure you rebound. And don't let anyone push you around out there," he said.

We huddled together and shouted a feisty, "Team!"

Walking onto the floor for the opening tip of the game was a who-could-give-the-dirtiest-look competition. Penny guarded Tasha because she knew I probably would have fouled out in the first quarter if I had played her. We scored first, and then we hit a long drought. For a while, I didn't think we were going to put four points on the board. The Hawks were everywhere.

"This is too easy," Tasha said after an easy basket.

My temperature rose, but there was nothing I could say. I looked up at the scoreboard at the beginning of the fourth quarter. We were down by 15 points. I wished that the clock would keep on running, just to put me out of my misery.

Penny managed to play well even though the rest of us didn't do much to help her. Rosie looked like a shrimp next to the Hawks. They pushed her around and beat her up all night.

"You all right, Rosie?" Angel asked.

Rosie didn't answer.

"Say something, would you!" Angel yelled.

"I'm fine," Rosie muttered as she rolled her eyes.

Wil acted like she was scared to death of Betsy Miner. She even apologized once when she fouled her.

"What are you doing?" I screamed.

"I hit her by accident," Wil said, and her eyes dropped to the ground.

"Don't go apologizing! She'll think you're scared of her."

"I didn't mean it..."

I just shook my head. I never had any trouble with body contact, especially in that game. I fouled out with two minutes left in the fourth quarter.

"Where's Sheila when you need her?" Tasha asked sarcastically as I passed her on the way to the bench. I turned to her and scowled.

"Molly!" Mr. Harris warned. I rolled my eyes and walked to the sideline. *Why did Tasha have to start? They won. What more did she want? Why did she have to go bullying people around all the time? Why was she so mean?*

"Just ignore her," Angel said as I passed her.

"Yeah, right," I shot back. "How can I? She's been yelling things in my face and pushing people around all night."

"Just let her go," Angel added calmly.

I sat down and folded my arms across my chest. My dad came into the gym seconds after I hit the bench. I felt his eyes on me. I kept my lips pursed. Then he took one look at the scoreboard and figured out for himself that there was little to say.

The buzzer finally sounded. We walked through the lines frowning, while the Hawks laughed and smiled.

"Nice try," Tasha snickered as she passed me.

"We'll see you again real soon," I said stubbornly.

I looked up at the scoreboard and didn't want to believe my eyes. The walloping was official. The final score read 44-22. Mr. Harris pulled us together.

"I don't want to see one of your heads looking down at the ground," he said sternly. "We will learn from this. You have to promise yourselves and each other that this will not happen again. Remember this feeling."

That was not a problem. Humiliation was something I always found easy to recall.

"Before I forget, Monday's practice will not be at Lincoln," he added. "Mr. Gordon arranged for us to scrimmage a team from Johnsville at their place. We'll be leaving at 6 p.m."

We threw our hands into a pile and yelled our customary, "Team!" It was weak.

"That's not good enough," Mr. Harris scolded. We did it again with phony enthusiasm.

I walked with Billy to our car.

"You'll do better next time," he said.

All I could do was groan.

"How's Frankie?" I asked my father.

"He's fine," he replied. "He has six stitches in his chin. The doctors and nurses had a heck of a time trying to keep him settled down. They had to put a straitjacket on him."

I laughed. Billy did too. It felt good to laugh.

When my dad and I walked into the house that night, Frankie was up watching television with Kevin.

"You okay, Frankie?" I asked.

He nodded.

"Did you win?" Kevin asked.

"No," I mumbled, "we got killed." I quickly changed the subject.

"Did the doctor let you keep the straitjacket, Frankie?" I asked. Everyone laughed except for Frankie, of course. Around our house, a crisis always turned into a joke after it became a thing of the past. I walked into the kitchen and sat with my dad at the table.

"I think playing against this team from Johnsville on Monday will be great for us," he said.

At any other time, I would have shown some sign of excitement, but not after what happened that night.

"Yeah," I mumbled.

"What happened tonight, Molls?" he asked.

"I don't know, Dad," I said lowly. "I just hate them."

"Don't use that word," my dad shot back.

Being a police officer, my father saw anger and violence every day. Coming home and hearing the word "hate" from one of his children hurt him as much as it angered him.

"Sorry," I mumbled, "I just dislike the Hawks very, very much. I wish they weren't so good."

"We have to get a lot better by the end of the summer to beat them," he said. "Do you think we can do it?"

I looked at him thoughtfully. "Do you think we can?" I asked.

He grinned. "Yes," he said confidently. "By the way you girls bounced back against those boys the other night, I know you can beat anyone."

I smiled. My dad always gave me hope. Then my mind flashed back to the Hawks. I suddenly felt guilty for not telling my father about fighting with Tasha. Maybe this would be a good time.

"Dad, I have to tell you something. But you've got to promise not to get mad," I bowed my head down and peered up with the saddest eyes I could possibly give him.

"It depends on what it is," he said cautiously. I had tried to lock him in on this promise thing before. He never went for it. But it was always worth another shot.

"When I told you that we saw the Hawks at the softball game last weekend, I didn't tell you everything," I said and then I paused. "We didn't just see them. I kind of got in a fight with one of them."

He stopped eating and the room fell silent.

"Molly, you know how I feel about you fighting," he raised his voice and tried to lock his eyes into mine. I dropped my head as he continued. "Sure, everybody gets mad and upset. But fighting? It makes no sense."

"But Tasha pushed Penny," I whined.

"And what did Penny do?" he asked.

"Nothing," I admitted.

"Which is exactly what you should have done," he answered.

"I couldn't just stand there and let her do that to Penny."

"Penny can handle herself. She knows better. I don't mind if you simply defend or protect yourself. But you shouldn't be starting anything. Ever. I don't want to hear that you've been fighting again. I mean it, Molly. Or else I'm taking you off the team for the summer."

"Come on, Dad," I persisted. "I shouldn't have even told you."

"Yes, you should have," he said and his voice rose again. "If I had found out from someone else, I would have taken you off the team immediately."

I could tell by his tone that he was serious. The thought of receiving such a punishment instantly stopped me from saying another word. He needed a long cooling off period. I brushed a kiss on his cheek, mumbled "good night," and moped into my bedroom feeling angry and frustrated.

It was all the Hawks' fault.

Chapter Eight

"This can't be it, Dad," I said as we all gazed out the window. The sights in Johnsville continued to amaze me. "It's way too big. It must be some college."

"These are the directions Mr. Gordon gave me," he assured me. "This is it." He parked the car and we all climbed out.

"One, two, three, four, five..." Wil counted the number of football, soccer, and baseball fields in sight. None of us could believe that one grade school and high school could add up to what was before our eyes. A vast wooded area surrounded clumps of buildings and playing fields, all of which were property of the Johnsville school system.

"I bet there are a lot of animals in those woods," Wil added.

"Lions, and tigers, and bears! Oh my!" Penny joked.

After some searching, we finally reached the correct wing of the grade school building. We weaved through the maze of spacious and freshly painted hallways, and peeked into the bright classrooms.

"Everyone grab a buddy, and make sure you don't lose that buddy," Angel said, mocking what our Lincoln teachers told us on field trips when we were younger.

When we walked through the gym doors, the movement and discussions of those inside came to a halt. Parents stopped gabbing with one another and stood silently as we passed along the baseline. There was not one greeting, and not one smile.

"Do we all have two heads?" whispered Wil.

Finally, the Johnsville coach jumped up from his bench and extended his hand to my father and to Mr. Harris. He told us where the locker room was and we followed his directions.

"What's with these people?" Angel muttered.

Penny and I swung open the locker room door and almost smacked into the two Johnsville girls coming out. They both jumped back.

"Oops," Penny said. "Sorry."

"This one is ours," one girl blurted out nervously. "That's yours," she said as she pointed to the next door.

"OK," Penny said softly. "Thanks."

Just before the door closed, I heard a low voice coming from inside.

"Don't leave anything in here."

Penny and I glanced blankly at each other for a brief second. *Did she say what I thought she said?* I looked to Penny for an explanation. Her eyes dropped and she turned away. *What kind of people did they think we were?* Penny ignored my begging eyes and continued on without a word.

In the locker room, Wil rummaged frantically through her bag. "Anybody got an extra pair of socks?" she asked. "I was in such a hurry I just slipped on my basketball shoes and forgot to throw some socks in my bag."

"Great, now your feet are going to stink all the way home," Angel said.

"You're riding in the other car," I added.

There was knock on the door. "Open up. It's us, girls," my dad said.

"Who's us?" Wil said.

"Open the door, Wil," Mr. Harris hollered, and she did as she was told. The coaches walked in. My dad looked down to Wil's feet.

"Where are your socks?" he asked.

"I forgot 'em."

"You want to borrow Frankie's?" my father offered.

Frankie barged into the locker room, dragging behind him the bag of basketballs. He was sweaty from running around outside. There were streaks of dirt across his cheek. My mom had made him wear a loose patch of gauze to keep the stitches on his chin clean.

"Ew," Wil replied. "No thanks, Mr. O."

Frankie simply shrugged his shoulders, dropped the bag, and scooted out the door.

I tucked in my shirt, and then grabbed at my neck. I forgot to take off my chain with the shamrock charm. My grandmother had given it to me when I was eight years old. I handed it to my dad, and he hooked it to his clipboard.

"Put it on right after the game is over," he ordered. He knew my mom told me to wear it only on special occasions, and how upset she would have been with me if she knew I had worn it to a basketball game.

"Grab a seat on the bench," Mr. Harris said. He glanced down the row of players, and stopped at Rosie. She had a deep purple shiner after getting smacked by a baseball during all-star practice.

"Rosie, it looks like you were boxing with Frankie," Mr. Harris quipped, and we all laughed.

"All right, settle down, girls," my father said.

The mood grew serious. Up until this point, not one person had dared to bring up the Hawks. The dreaded time had come.

"We weren't too pleased with how you all played on Friday night. The Hawks are a good team, a really good team. But we can beat them. Do you want to beat them?"

No one knew whether to answer or not.

"Yeah," Wil grumbled.

"Do you want to beat them?" my dad repeated louder.

"Yeah!" we all shouted.

"In order to do that, we must gain something from each practice and each game. Are you ready to play?"

"Yes!" we all screamed with conviction. A wave of a fresh emotion spilled over us. We huddled up and jogged out of the locker room.

The crowd of what looked like parents and families nearly doubled while we were in the locker room. It seemed like it was some kind of championship game, and everyone knew about it except us. My eyes picked through the stands, and I noticed one black man sitting in a crowd of mostly white people. It was our principal, Mr. Gordon. He winked, and I smiled. It felt good to see a familiar face.

The game started. Within the first couple of minutes, I knew there was something strange going on. There was something different about playing Johnsville compared to when we played against other teams from the city. Every time Johnsville did something good, the bench erupted and the fans cheered wildly. Passionately. They were crazy. It was as if it was more than just a game. After one basket, I looked to my dad for an explanation.

"Play hard, Blue!" he cried out. "Play hard!"

During a free throw, I took a good look at Rosie's black eye. It was a nasty one. Then I looked at sockless Wil in her drenched blue T-shirt. Our Ballplayers T-shirts hadn't come in yet, so we all decided to wear navy blue or the closest color we had to it. Wil wore one of her father's old shirts, which had a rip in the sleeve after our game against Sheila. Next to the Johnsville girls, who were decked out in their sharp green and white uniforms with their names printed on their backs, we looked like a bunch of ragamuffins.

At half-time, we were up by 10 points. But by the end of the third quarter, Johnsville had come within three points of us. They put two players on Penny every time she crossed half-court.

"Pass it around," Mr. Harris yelled.

A Johnsville girl stole the ball from me, and I sprinted madly next to her as she dribbled to the other end for a lay-up. I jumped up to block the shot, and I bumped into her body. She exaggerated her fall, and collapsed to the ground dramatically. I threw my arms up claiming my innocence. The referee blew his whistle as hard as he could and came running with his hand pointing right at me. I dropped my hands down helplessly as the crowd tore into me.

"Get her out of there!" a woman yelled.

"Intentional!" another guy screamed.

I wanted to cry. *How could they think I meant to do it? What did they think I was?*

Penny came up to me. "Take it easy, Molly," she whispered.

"I didn't mean it," I yelled.

"I know," she said softly. Penny's understanding eyes looked as if she had been through this before. "But you can't get away with anything here. You gotta be smart."

The Johnsville players shot dirty looks at me. Suddenly my hurt turned into anger. I looked to my dad, hoping for some logical explanation. I read his lips. "It's OK, Molls," he said. "Hang in there."

It wasn't OK, but I hung in there anyway. The next trip down, Wil picked up her fifth foul.

"Yes!" A Johnsville fan cheered. "Way to go, Green!"

"Warm up the bus," a kid yelled sarcastically. "And go home!"

Right then it all became clear. We were the rough, tough, mean city kids. Kids that would steal your clothes if you left them behind or beat you up if you were walking alone. That's why they were cheering so hard. We weren't the opponent. We were the criminals.

"Good game, Wil," I screamed madly. "Good game."

With 30 seconds left, we were up by one. The Johnsville girls slowed the game down. Their plan was to pass the ball around for a long time hoping we would grow impatient and make a stupid, crucial mistake.

"No fouls, no fouls!" Mr. Harris shouted from the sideline. My girl finally drove to the basket, and I knew not to foul her. I beat her to where she was going, and threw my arms up perfectly straight. She leaned into me and tossed up prayer. It careened off the backboard and she fell to the ground. The whistle shrieked. With four seconds left, the referee called the foul on me.

"What?" my dad screamed.

My fifth foul made the crowd ecstatic. I trudged down the sideline. My face felt hot and my insides still hurt. If I looked at my dad, I would have started to cry. So I ignored him and sat alone at the end of the bench. I watched helplessly as the Johnsville girl who ran into me, made two free throws to win the game. When the final buzzer sounded, the players and fans celebrated wildly.

"It wasn't fair!" I shouted to my dad. He grabbed my shoulder, and I wrestled free of his grip. I stomped off toward the locker room.

"Shake their hands, Molly," he said sternly.

"No," I shot back. "What's wrong with these people?"

"Molly," his voice rose threateningly.

I turned and trudged through the line without looking one player in the eye. I unhooked my necklace from my dad's clipboard, and stood by the door. I had enough of Johnsville.

I looked up and saw Mr. Liberty, the man who hosted our school pool party, and the one who helped Mr. Gordon set up the scrimmage against Johnsville. As he walked down the stands with Mr. Gordon, he called all the coaches together. I watched carefully as Mr. Gordon did most of the talking. *You tell 'em, Mr. G. Tell 'em they're rotten and unfair. You tell 'em!*

Mr. Harris whistled and we trudged over. The Johnsville coach rounded up his players too. I was certain that Mr. Gordon was going to let everyone have it.

"I just want to say that both teams played a great game," Mr. Liberty began.

"And I wanted to invite the Johnsville girls to Lincoln for a scrimmage next week," Mr. Gordon said.

What? My mouth dropped. Mr. Gordon looked into my wide eyes but he kept talking. "Around 7:00 or 7:30?"

"Seven-thirty works for us," the Johnsville coach answered. His players were speechless.

"I thought we'd order some pizzas and head over to the club before you girls went home," Mr. Liberty said. "Pizza is on Mr. Gordon." he added laughing.

I rolled my eyes at the absurdity of it all. It made no sense. I began to wonder if it was all some kind of practical joke.

"I'm hungry," Wil said.

"Me too," Angel added.

I was convinced that everyone around me was either blind, deaf, or just plain dumb.

"I don't want to go, Dad," I whispered to him as the crowd broke up.

"You have no choice."

"I'm really tired," I said. "I'll just sit in the car."

"You will not," he warned. "That would be rude. Mr. Liberty is a good friend of Mr. Gordon's. And Mr. Gordon has always been good to us."

"Did you see how they treated us?"

He nodded his head. "It made me angry. But it doesn't do any good to treat them the same way they treated you."

"I don't care," I shot back. "They don't like us. They don't even want us here."

"That's enough," he shot back, and his face turned red.

It was a no-win situation. I didn't feel like walking home, which is what my dad would have made me do if I dared to stay in the car.

The Country Club was five minutes down the road. When we arrived, Angel and I jumped out the back window of the station wagon to escape the stench of Wil's feet.

"You better hope that Mr. Liberty lets you take a swim and wash off those feet before we go home," Angel said.

We walked into the dining room, and sat at our own table separate from the Johnsville players. I wasn't exactly in the mood to mingle. When Mr. Gordon called my name, I wanted to pretend I didn't hear him. But I couldn't. He waved me toward him and I dragged myself over.

"Molly, I'd like you to meet Jane," Mr. Gordon said.

"Jane is Mr. Liberty's niece." I eyed her suspiciously. She was the one who made the two free throws to beat us. I didn't say anything.

"Molly, why don't you and I go get a couple sodas. Excuse us, please," Mr. Gordon added sternly.

"You better start talking, young lady," he said grimly as we walked. I was so deep into trouble that I just didn't care anymore. The words flew up my throat so fast I wanted to scream. Somehow I remembered who I was talking to. I took one deep breath, and out of respect for Mr. Gordon, I used a loud, angry whisper.

"Did you see what they did to us? How they treated us? How they thought we wanted to steal their things, and beat them up?

"Yes," he said softly.

"Didn't you hear what those parents said to me, and how they cheered when Wil fouled out?"

He nodded his head.

"And you don't even care," I muttered.

Mr. Gordon paused and took a deep breath. "Now Molly, are you and the rest of your friends anything like what they think of you?"

"Of course not," I snapped.

"Well, how are they supposed to know that?"

"I don't know," I mumbled.

"Maybe if you get to know each other you'll be able to show them that you are not like what they think. And you'll probably see that some of the girls might not think like some of their parents do. You've got to give them a chance, and they will give you one, too."

I didn't answer. I was too busy mulling over what he had said. We eached grabbed two cans of soda and walked back over to Mr. Liberty and Jane.

"Molly," Mr. Liberty said. "Mr. Gordon tells me you love to swim. Jane loves the water too. Do you girls want to go for a swim?"

Jane's eyes lit up, and she eagerly awaited my response. I wasn't about to cooperate.

"We didn't bring our suits," I muttered.

"You can use some of our extra T-shirts and shorts," Jane said excitedly. "We always have some old clothes in the lost and found box. That's what we usually wear when we forget our suits."

I didn't want to give a straight answer. I was still damaged by the loss. And being stuck at the country club was a reminder of all the horrible things that I saw and heard that night. I didn't want to go swimming. I wanted to go home.

Then Mr. Gordon's glaring eyes got a hold of me.

"All right," I finally mumbled. "Wil needs a swim. She forgot her socks and her feet stink." Mr. Liberty burst into a hearty laugh, which irritated me. I wasn't trying to be funny.

Jane pulled out the box of extra T-shirts and shorts, and we headed to the locker room. Some of the girls from Johnsville didn't have their suits.

"Is it OK if we change in here, too?" one asked as she stuck her head in the locker room.

"Come on in!" Penny yelled. "We wouldn't make you go in the boys' room." Penny cracked some jokes, while we took turns using the stalls to change out of our clothes. The Johnsville girls started to laugh and talk. When Penny didn't change out of her uniform, one girl asked why she wasn't swimming.

"I don't swim at night," Penny said. "It's too cold."

"Yeah, right," Rosie mumbled.

"Penny doesn't swim," I expained.

"I'll be the lifeguard tonight for everyone," Penny added.

"I feel safe," Angel laughed.

I unhooked my necklace and set it down on the bench next to my shoes. "That's pretty," Jane said. "I'm Irish, too."

I half-smiled and then I turned away. Wil and I raced out of the locker room, and put on the brakes just before we hit the pool deck and slowed down. Wil, Jane and I lined up with our toes curled over the end of the pool.

"On three, we all jump," Wil said.

"You better, Wil!" I called out.

"One...two...three!"

I sprung off my feet, and so did Jane. I looked over my shoulder and screamed, "Wil!" I saw her bend over laughing just as I broke the surface. I held my breath as I shot up from underwater.

"Gotcha!" Wil said. Jane and I swung our arms out of the water and splashed her.

We set up relay races and played pool games. Wil started a synchronized swimming demonstration by dancing dramatically outside the pool and then lowering herself into the water.

"It's synchronized swimming, starring Funky Feet!" Penny bellowed. Not one person could hold a straight face as Wil flailed through her routine.

The pizza came, and we had a contest to see which team could eat the most slices. We won easily. Wil, Anita and I almost beat the Johnsville girls by ourselves.

"What's your record?" I asked Jane after we were finished eating.

"We're something like 7-1," she said. "I'm not really sure. But most of the teams aren't as good as you. We played earlier in the spring together, and now we just play whatever games we can. What's yours?"

"We're 1-1 in our league," Penny said. "This is the first summer league for us."

"Where do you play all the games?" Jane asked.

"At our school or at the park district gyms," Penny said.

"I haven't been in the city that much," Jane said. "What's it like?"

"You don't have to be scared if that's what you're thinking," I said defensively.

"I'm not," she snapped back. "I just don't know what it's like, that's all."

"We just live a little closer together than you all. We don't get as many fans at our games like you, and our gym is a lot smaller," Penny said.

"Don't you get scared out here with all the animals in the woods?" asked Wil.

Jane laughed.

"I'm serious," Wil said.

"No. There's nothing to be scared of except some opossums and raccoons if you leave your garbage out. And maybe some deer. But they're friendly."

"Aren't you afraid that someone is going to jump out of the bushes and get you? In the city, if you screamed, at least somebody would hear you."

"Whether or not they would do something about it is a different story," Penny added.

"It's not like that at all," Jane said. "You should come stay at my house sometime."

"I need noise though," Wil said. "I'll bring my radio."

"You should come to our park," Penny said. "You could play ball with us sometime and maybe come to one of our games."

"Yeah," Wil agreed. "You can come when we play the Hawks."

"The Hawks?" Jane asked.

"Yeah," Penny said. "They beat us last Friday night."

"They're a bunch of..." I couldn't finish my sentence. Mr. Gordon was approaching our table.

"How's the pizza, girls?" he asked. By then, a couple of other Johnsville girls had sat down with us.

"Good," we replied. I refused to look at him.

"Is everyone having a good time?" he asked.

"Yeah," Wil said as Rosie nodded. I continued to look the other away.

A short time later, my dad walked over and told us that we had to go. We cleaned up our mess, and changed our clothes.

"Thanks for the swim, Mr. Liberty," Penny called out.

"The Ballplayers are welcome anytime," he replied.

We yelled good-bye to the Johnsville girls as Mr. Liberty and Mr. Gordon walked us to the parking lot. Just before I slipped into the car, Jane came running out of breath to catch up to us.

"Molly, Molly," she gasped. "You forgot your necklace."

I thanked Jane, and stepped in the car. As I hooked my shamrock charm around my neck, I peeked up at Mr. Gordon through the window. I managed one faint smile. He winked, and watched us drive off into the night.

Chapter Nine

I cringed when I saw Eddie slip through the doorway at our practice on Monday night. He couldn't just torment me for a mere five or six hours at the park during the day. Now the bully had taken the night shift as well to be an official, full-time pain in my neck.

Unfortunately, Eddie was the least of our concerns. We didn't have a full team again. Jessica and Mary had pulled another no-show, and Wil was out of town. As we finished up our last shooting drill, the fathers finally broke from a strategy discussion on the sideline. My big ears told me the topic was Beef Potato. With Wil absent, the question that lingered was who would guard him.

The boys only had four players until J.J. burst through the door.

"Hey, hey," he said as he strut onto the floor. "I heard ya'll needed some competition."

"Well, why didn't you bring any?" Penny joked. We all laughed, and even J.J. struggled to conceal his grin.

"Who's gonna guard Beef?" Penny asked.

Everyone looked around at each other hoping someone would volunteer.

"I will," Rosie said and she shrugged her thin shoulders and smiled up at us. We all started laughing again.

Mr. Harris called out the match-ups. "Molly, you take J. Penny, you guard Mike. Angel you take Eddie. Rosie, you've got Marvin, and Anita, you have Beef."

"Ugh," Anita moaned.

Our six-foot tall center had to know it was coming. We had no other alternative. She was the only one who stood a chance at wrestling with Beef's strength and skill.

"Be tough," Mr. Harris told her as we all walked out on the floor.

Beef, as usual, played solid and respectable basketball. He hustled and scrapped for every rebound. When J.J. started lighting it up from the outside, it lessened Beef's workload underneath.

"Get a hand up on J!" my dad yelled at me. I did and J.J. simply passed it inside to Beef for a lay-up.

"Come on girls!" Mr. Jones screamed. I hadn't seen Rosie's father walk in the gym. But we all heard him loud and clear.

"Make a shot, Rosie! Dribble! Oh, come on! Keep your head up!"

I looked over at Rosie. Her eyes fell to the ground. *Why did he have to be so hard on her?* We were all trying our best. I hated when coaches and parents went crazy on the sidelines. It was embarrassing. I never understood how people could think shouting angry words would make someone play better.

"You got it, Rosie," I said. "Nice try."

The next play down court, Beef grabbed a rebound and turned to outlet the ball to Eddie. His sharp elbow caught poor Anita square in the chin. She screamed and buckled over. My dad sprinted out onto the floor. Beef stood over her with his hand resting on her back. I thought he was gonna cry.

"I'm sorry, I'm sorry," Beef gasped. "I didn't mean it, Mr. O. Honest."

"It's all right, Beef," my dad assured him.

Anita was still in one piece, but a bit shook up. She sat out, which left us with no substitutions.

"Who's gonna guard Beef?" Penny asked.

"Fall into a zone girls," my dad said. I groaned in disappointment. I wanted to be the one to guard Beef.

"Molly, line up on the right side," my dad commanded. "That's Beef's favorite side. Guard him tough when he's there, and the others will help you."

I proudly nodded my head not knowing what I was getting myself into. Despite using all of my power and might, Beef shook me off like a pathetic weakling.

"Box him out, Molly!" my dad yelled, which only irritated me further. Beef was too big and strong for me to box out.

"I can't!" I screamed back.

"You can!" Mr. Harris shot back. "We don't talk like that!"

Whatever. I was trying my best. But nothing worked. In one last attempt to reassert myself, I barreled my way to the basket on the offensive end. Eddie jumped out of nowhere, stretched out his body, and cleanly pinned the ball to my arm just before I had a chance to let it go. The force with which he pressed the ball down sent me flailing to the ground.

"Get it outta here," Eddie snarled. I peeled myself up off the ground. I shot him a dirty look, and then dropped my head down.

There was nothing quite like ending a horrible practice with such a humiliating moment.

• • • •

The boys had crushed us that night. At the park the next day, Eddie replayed blocking my shot at least a half-a-dozen times.

"Betcha you'll think twice before you take it to the bucket on me again," he said.

"Face it, Eddie, you were lucky," I said.

"You're so weak," he said.

"Shut up," I said. "You're the one who's weak."

"Don't let him get to you," Penny said softly to me.

"You're so weak my little sister could beat you in a game of one-on-one," he said.

"Yeah, right," I mumbled. "You're such a loser, Eddie."

"He's getting to you," Penny muttered.

I ignored her.

"You're such a girl," Eddie shot back.

I picked up my ball and threw it at him as hard as I could. He slid out of the way, and the ball went flying past. He laughed obnoxiously. "Nice throw!" he snickered. Penny just stood shaking her head.

"Jerk!" I called out to Eddie. Just when I felt like slugging him, I recalled my dad's words about taking me off the team if he caught me fighting again. I wondered if that included Eddie. I didn't want to take a chance, so I forced myself to cool down. I just insulted him a couple more times, and he did the same.

"Maybe we should find a way to lower the basket for you, Molly," he said.

"Maybe you should shut up," I shot back.

The conversation was going nowhere, and Penny was getting tired of it.

"Let's go then," Penny said. Her eyes locked into Eddie's. "Let's play. You, J.J., and Billy against me, Molly, and Rosie.

"Ball is in," Penny called out, and she checked the ball to Eddie.

Rosie and I scurried into our positions. Penny Harris didn't get upset too many times. But she was tired of losing, and tired of arguing. She wanted some peace and quiet. On some days, the only way we could get that at the park was to just play.

Penny moved right and left with the same fluidness. She stopped and popped the jumper for one score, and tossed a no-look pass to me for the next basket.

"Yo, Eddie," J.J. said lowly, hoping not to embarrass him too much. "Let me guard her."

"I got her!" Eddie screamed back.

Penny ran the show. Eddie couldn't stop her, and neither could J.J. After a couple of minutes, the score was 14-9 in our favor. Rosie made a steal, and then passed the ball to Penny. Penny hit me for a lay-up, which ended the game.

"Yes!" Penny said as the ball went through the net. She jogged up to me and slapped my hand.

"Thanks," I muttered knowing Penny really didn't need me. She gave me the ball for the last shot just to make sure I felt important. Penny could have beaten Eddie, J.J., and Billy all by herself.

• • • •

By the time Friday night's game rolled around, I thought we had recovered from both losses to Johnsville and the boys. But I thought wrong.

We moped into the locker room at half-time and sunk down onto the bench. We were losing to the Kingsley Royals by 10 points, and it didn't even feel that close. Then we started arguing, which made things worse.

"Nobody's playing any defense," Angel said.

"We gotta pass the ball," Wil added.

"We gotta catch it, too," I said. Wil had dropped two passes.

"I'm trying," Wil whined.

"Stop arguing," Rosie muttered.

We all turned and looked at our shy friend. When she spoke, we had to listen, because we didn't know when it would happen again.

"If everybody would just play and stop yelling at each other, we'll win," she added.

Rosie's soft words made us stop and think. The few seconds of peace and quiet gave us a chance to catch our breaths. Everyone was searching for answers. I took one look at my furious dad as he marched in the locker room, and knew that he was going to blow.

"You are not playing the way you are capable of!" my dad's voice boomed. My insides tightened. I hated when he yelled like that, especially in front of my friends. "So what if you got killed by the Hawks and lost a close one to Johnsville. That's no excuse to completely fall apart the way you are right now. Stop feeling sorry for yourselves and get out there and play some real basketball!"

The second half was slightly better, but we were too busy playing catch-up. With only six players, we lacked the punch we needed at the end. We lost by six, which stuck us with an overall record of one win and two losses.

Not much was said after the game except when Penny asked when the Johnsville girls were coming to play against us at Lincoln.

"On Monday," my dad replied. "The scrimmage starts at 7:30."

There wasn't much conversation on the car ride home either. It was one of those difficult moments where mutual empty feelings spoke more than words could say.

After we dropped Anita off at her house, Annie asked, "Why is everyone so quiet, Dad?"

"We're just upset because we didn't play well," he replied.

"You only lost by six," Annie said, and she held up six fingers and counted them with her eyes.

She was young. She didn't understand why we were down. It had been a long week. And summer league had only just begun.

Chapter Ten

On Monday night, we started a mini-practice at 7 p.m. sharp.

"Lay-up lines, girls," my dad said before I even had a chance to untie the ballbag.

"Come on, Dad," I whined.

"Let's go, Molls," he said. "Johnsville is going to be here soon."

I began to sense that both of our coaches had also taken the Johnsville loss personally.

"Let's concentrate tonight on taking good shots and making them," Mr. Harris called out.

We ran through our usual lay-up drill where we had to get seven in a row on each side. On a bad shooting night, the drill took no more than 10 minutes.

That night was a different story. We suddenly became a different team. I looked up to the clock on the wall. At least 10 minutes had passed, and we hadn't even passed three consecutive lay-ups on the right side alone. Something strange was happening to us. Our smiles disappeared, and everyone started rolling their eyes. We huffed and groaned after misses. Every shot became a chore.

A strident whistle snapped us still.

"Hold it," Mr. Harris yelled. "That's it!" He shook his head. "What bothers me more than anything is not the losing. It's the sulking. You girls have worked too hard to be standing around with your heads down. If you can't play with any pride, then you shouldn't be out here."

All eyes remained locked to the ground. No one moved. We had never heard Mr. Harris raise his voice in such frustration. My father was usually the one who did all the yelling.

"The rest of the practice time and the scrimmage is yours," Mr. Harris said. He walked to the sideline and sat on the bleachers.

"It's up to you to work hard and to believe in yourselves," my father said. "You owe it to each other." He walked off the court shaking his head. The silence was deafening. I was so frustrated that I wanted to cry. It was downright rotten for two grown adults to abandon a bunch of discouraged kids when they couldn't feel any lower.

"What do we do?" Wil whispered.

"We play on our own," Penny shot back.

"Yeah," Angel added.

"Forget them," I said. I suddenly was mad at them for leaving us. All of us were. Penny extended her arm out and pulled me next to her. She grabbed Wil's hand and slapped it on top of hers. We huddled up, and all eyes fell on our natural born leader.

"Let's show them and let's show each other that we're much better than this," Penny said softly so our fathers couldn't hear.

"Let's cheer for each other," Angel continued.

"Yeah," Rosie said. "No more yelling."

"Team on three," Penny said. "One, two, three...Team!"

We shouted with determination, and sprinted back into our lay-up lines. I cheered extra loud for everyone, just as Angel asked. I looked around the floor, and watched scowling faces smile again. Soon soft-touched lay-ups accompanied our cheers. My friends and I were back.

"Way to go, Blue!" Angel screamed.

While the Johnsville girls and parents filtered in the gym, Angel kept us in line and concentrating. I waved quickly at Jane. There was no time to talk.

In the meantime, our coaches had been laughing and chatting on the sidelines. It was as if there was nothing abnormal or wrong with the situation they had created. Frankie hit the horn, and set the scoreboard. Little Sammy and Annie collected all the basketballs and slid them into the ball bag. We walked briskly over to the bench, and waited for the coaches. But when they sat down and deliberately ignored us, we quickly realized that they were serious.

"I thought we were supposed to be the immature ones," Wil whispered.

Penny and I looked at each other and shrugged our shoulders. Before anyone had a chance to say anything more, Angel took over.

"Penny, Anita, Molly, Rosie, and Wil—you're in," she said. We gulped down some water and jogged onto the floor.

The Johnsville girls won the tip. I picked off a ball, and passed it ahead to Penny who was already down the floor. She took three hard dribbles and made her lay-up.

"Way to play, Molly!" she called out.

Wil grabbed a rebound, and passed it to Rosie. She brought the ball up the floor, and we passed it around to one another. Then Rosie dribbled down the middle and passed the ball to Anita for a wide-open shot.

"Nice pass!" Anita yelled as she ran back on defense.

We controlled the first quarter like never before. The Johnsville parents sat in a stunned silence. I glanced over to my dad. When he smiled approvingly, I turned away. I was still mad at him for being so stubborn.

The Johnsville girls got into the swing of things in the second quarter, but our 6-0 spurt in the last two minutes gave us the momentum and confidence going into half-time. We jogged into the locker room screaming and yelling like wild animals.

I turned to Rosie and even caught her screaming. She reached her hand out and I slapped her a high five.

"Way to go, Blue!" she cheered.

Angel settled us down. "All right," she said, "let's do the same thing in the second half."

I could see the emotion in her eyes. Angel was fired up.

"We can do it!" she said. "Play good defense and keep passing to each other."

We filled up our water bottles and walked onto the court. Our coaches still did not move from their spots on the bench.

"Are you ever coming back, or is it over for good?" Wil asked slyly as she walked past them.

"You don't need us," Mr. Harris said smiling.

"Yes we do," Wil said. She stopped and looked at the scoreboard thoughtfully. We were winning 20-8.

"Maybe it looks like we don't need you right now. But who's going to take us out for pizza after the tough games on Friday nights?"

My dad laughed. "It's up to Angel," he said. "She's done such a nice job coaching. We don't want to just take over on her."

"No, Mr. O.," Angel assured him. "It's all yours. Coaching isn't for me. Can I get some playing time?"

Our coaches stood up and rejoined our huddle. We rolled through the game and won 32-14.

After walking past the other team in the traditional hand-shaking line, Jane stopped to talk to me.

"Nice game, Molly," she said sincerely. "Your team was different tonight. What have you been doing during the week?"

"Losing," I admitted, "and we got sick of it."

"I guess so," she said shaking her head.

"I asked my parents if you could stay over this weekend," I said. "Penny and Wil and Angel and Rosie are staying, too. You wanna come over?"

Jane eyes grew wide. "Sure," she said.

"Maybe you can come to our game on Friday night," I said.

"OK," she said cheerfully. "Hold on. I've gotta ask my mom." Jane darted away and interrupted her mother, who was talking with another woman. I watched Jane's mom hesitate and take a deep breath. Jane tugged on her arm. Her mother told her something and then nodded. Jane sprinted back.

"She said it's OK, but she wants to meet your mom or dad first," she blurted between breaths.

Wil and I started shooting around with Jane and her teammate, Amy, while the coaches and parents mingled.

"Let's play some three-on-three," Wil suggested.

"Shoot for teams," Penny said.

It ended up Jane, Amy and me against Rosie, Penny, and Wil. No one kept score. We just played, and laughed, and sweat until our parents threatened to leave without us.

"Mr. O," Penny shouted. "Can we play the best of seven?"

"Only if you're all sleeping on the streets tonight," he said.

Penny's mother picked up the ball and started dribbling onto the floor. Both my mother and Penny's mother worked at the city hospital. And both of them always traded shifts with other nurses so they could come and watch us play. Watching wasn't the only thing they liked to do. Mrs. Harris started smiling as she looked up at the basket.

It had to go in. Even if Mrs. Harris never touched a ball in her life, I was convinced that her shot was going to go in.

It did. Mrs. Harris smiled proudly as little Sammy chased after the ball.

"Let's go," Mrs. Harris said. "I shot 100 percent for the night. I'm gonna quit while I'm ahead."

Penny sunk one last jumper. She and little Sammy waved good-bye as they jogged out the door.

"I'm leaving," Jane's mom said. "I guess you're walking home. It's a long way back to Johnsville."

Jane said good-bye, and she scooted out the door in front of her mother.

"Call me tomorrow," I yelled.

My mother walked out onto the court and grabbed a rebound. She decided it was her turn. After seeing Mrs. Harris do it, I was betting that my mom thought she could do it, too. But little did she know how easy everyone in Penny's family made basketball seem. My mother shot-putted the ball up at the basket so hard that she almost broke the backboard.

"Oh, Ma," I groaned in embarrassment. She chased down her ridiculous shot, and chucked up another sorry attempt. I winced.

"A little softer," I suggested.

I felt a heavy hand on my shoulder.

"I see where you get your strength and toughness from," Mr. Gordon said.

I shrugged, not knowing if being compared to my mom at that moment was a good or bad thing.

"She never had a chance to play like you and your friends do now," he explained. "Maybe you could teach her a thing or two."

"I guess it's never too late to start," I said as I winced at her final attempt which banked off the top of the square. I picked up the ball, and my mom held her hands up for me to pass it back to her. I faked a pass to her, and tucked the ball under my arm as I walked off the court.

"Come on, Molly," she pleaded as she laughed, "Just one more?"

"No, mom," I said grinning. "It's late, and we've got to go." I looked down and massaged my ball. "I think you bruised it."

She laughed, and then rounded everyone up. The boys were moving in.

"Dad, can I stay and play?" I asked.

"No," he said, "let's just go home. You've played enough today."

"Please?" I begged.

"No, Molly. Mom doesn't have to work. Everybody is going to be home tonight."

I gave in and followed my family out the door.

• • • •

Later that night, my father made some popcorn while we watched a late movie. I fell asleep not even half-way through, and woke up when I felt my dad's hand on my back.

"It's time for bed," he whispered.

He walked me into my room and tucked me in next to Annie, who was already fast asleep.

"I was extra proud of you tonight," he whispered. "You and the girls came together."

"Why did you do that to us, Dad?" I moaned with my eyes closed. "Why'd you quit on us?"

"We didn't quit on you." He kept his voice low. "It might be best for me to let you go sometimes. So you can see for yourself that you can do things on your own," he paused. "Are you still mad at me, Molls?" he asked.

"No," I grumbled, "I was just afraid for a second that you weren't coming back."

"I would never leave you, Molls," he said. "I'm your biggest fan."

A lump formed in my throat. What he said made my insides gush. I opened my eyes and smiled at him.

"Good night, Molly," he whispered. He kissed me on the cheek and then left my room. I squeezed my pillow tight and said a prayer for my father, my family, and for all my friends before I fell asleep.

Chapter Eleven

When the final buzzer sounded on the following Friday night, we treated our win as if it were business as usual. There was too little time and too much to be done. We coolly walked through the hand-slapping lines, and headed into the locker room. After we changed into our T-shirts, Penny and I walked over to Jane, who had sat with Annie and little Sammy during the game.

"It must of killed you to sit there and just watch," I said to her. "I can't handle sitting in the stands. It drives both of us nuts." I waved my finger, pointing at Penny and myself.

"Can we shoot some before we go?" she asked.

"Sure," Penny said.

"I'll get a ball," Annie offered. She hustled over to the bench and grabbed a ball.

"What's your record now?" Jane asked me.

"We're 2-2 in the league with three games left. We lost last Friday night. We kind of beat ourselves. But the Hawks, well, they beat us by themselves. And by a lot."

"What's with these Hawks that everyone is talking about?" Jane asked.

I didn't want to get myself all worked up, so I let Penny answer that question.

"They're tough," Penny admitted. "A couple of them are some of the biggest and strongest girls in the city."

"That's not why we can't stand them," I added, trying to at least sound fair.

"It's that they know they're good," Penny continued. "And they're not afraid to go around telling it to people and rubbing it in other teams' faces."

"They're a bunch of bullies," Wil yelled from the sideline, "and they're not afraid to fight. Just ask Molly."

All eyes were on me. The words rushed up my throat, and then got stuck just before I almost blurted them out. It was impossible for me to explain why I fought. I would have sounded stupid and foolish trying to justify myself so I didn't say anything. I peeked up at Jane, and her disapproving eyes crushed me. I suddenly felt like a brute.

"I don't fight anymore," I mumbled.

"Yeah, sure," Wil said sarcastically.

"I don't," I shot back. "Well, I can't. Not anymore. My dad said he would take me off the team if he heard about me fighting again."

"So that's why you've been good," Penny called out in disbelief. "Even when Eddie was bugging you last week?"

"It's no big deal," I mumbled. I was lying. Me walking away from a fight was like Wil refusing one of my mother's cupcakes. It just didn't happen. I purposely changed the subject. "Penny, is this the week that you're going to visit your grandma?"

"Yeah," she said.

It was the only game I truly dreaded. Wil and I looked at each other apprehensively, knowing how hard it would be to play without Penny on Friday night.

"Looks like I'll have to carry the team," Wil joked, and I rolled my eyes.

"Let's go, girls," my dad hollered, and he hustled us out of the gym. Our weekly Friday night movie began at 9 p.m., and we were already running late.

"Let me grab my bag," Jane said, "and remind me to call my mom before it gets too late."

We rushed home and dropped our sweaty bodies on the living room floor after my dad warned us not to sit on the new furniture. Penny popped some popcorn during commercial breaks, while the rest of us lounged around the living room in front of the TV.

"What do you think of the city?" Angel asked Jane.

"It's noisy," she said.

"Are you scared to be here?" Wil asked curiously.

"No," Jane said and her eyes turned down. "Do I look scared?"

Nobody answered, which told me that we all felt the same feelings that night we were playing in Johnsville.

"Well, not now," I said. "But the first time we walked in your gym, it seemed as if everyone was scared of us because we were from the city. Like you were thinking bad stuff."

"I wasn't," Jane said.

"Not you," I continued, "but lots of other people on your team and in the stands were. They yelled some pretty mean things."

"I know," Jane said and her eyes dropped down. "I hope you don't think that I think that way."

"You don't," Wil said firmly, "because if you did, you wouldn't be here right now."

"Jane—don't forget to call your mom," Rosie remembered.

"Oh yeah, thanks," Jane said, and she picked up the phone.

"Hi, mom," she said and paused. "I'm at Molly's. They won." Jane didn't say much more than that for the next minute except for the occasional yes and no.

"I'm fine mom," she whispered. "Don't worry."

After she hung up, I looked at Jane suspiciously.

"Is she worried about you being in the city with us?" I asked.

"She's not worried about being with you, but she is worried about me being away from home," admitted Jane. "I just told her not to worry."

I stopped being so defensive, and realized that there was no sense in holding anything against Jane. The problem was beyond us.

"I'm starving," Angel said as the aroma of buttered popcorn grew heavier.

"Me, too," Wil added. "It smells so good."

Penny walked into the living room with her arms wrapped around a large wooden bowl. Annie followed behind her with a stack of smaller ones.

We filled our bellies with soda and popcorn as we chatted and laughed through the movie and late into the night. After only about six hours of sleep, we grabbed some muffins for breakfast, and headed down to the park.

"Welcome to Anderson Park," J.J. called out to Jane. "It's our park. And there's no other place on this earth quite like it."

I'm sure after all our hype Jane must have been slightly disappointed by what she saw. The swing set begged for a paint job, and the water fountain had overflowed into a big runny puddle. The nets on the baskets were frayed and torn.

"Yo, J!" Penny yelled across the court. "We got next!"

A smile peeped out of Jane, and then hid back inside. She knew we had accepted her as one of us. And she didn't want to disappoint the group by being anything less than cool on the courts.

We lost our first game, and then pulled ourselves together. Once we started winning, we couldn't stop. By noon, we had defeated every team that had stepped on the court for over an hour.

"Let's run it back," J.J. said bitterly after we beat his team again.

"I'm done, J," Mike said.

"Come on," J.J. pleaded.

"It's too hot, man," Mike replied. "I'm about to pass out."

"Let's get outta here," Wil said. "There's no competition here today, anyway."

"What's the matter?" J.J. said. "You hungry?"

"Cut it out, J," I yelled.

"I'm hot," Angel said. "Let's take a break."

We walked off the courts and stood under the one tree in the middle of the park.

"We need some air-conditioning," Wil mumbled.

"Let's go to the show," Penny offered. "Then we can come back later if we want."

"What do you want to do, Jane?" I asked.

Jane looked beat. Her face was sun-burned and her white shirt was stained with dirt. "I don't care either way," she said.

"Come on, Molly. Please?" Wil pleaded. "We can sit in a nice cool theater."

"All right," I said.

"Maybe my brother can drive us," Rosie said. "I'll go home and ask him. Then I'll call you."

"I'm outta here," Wil said. "Let's meet at Molly's house in half-an-hour." We walked back up to Broadway Ave., and then split off into the directions of our houses.

After a change of clothes and a bite to eat, Rosie's older brother, Rico, picked us up at my house. Angel was brushing her hair as we walked down the driveway.

"Would you stop with the hair," Wil said. "You're driving me crazy."

Angel smiled and then she shrugged. She jammed her brush in her back pocket. Then she took out her ribbon and fixed her hair.

"Here she goes with the bow," Penny called out.

We laughed as we piled into Rico's midnight blue Mustang and cruised through the city. The music was blaring.

"Rosie," I asked, "is Rico still playing baseball?"

"He's waiting to hear about going to a camp," she replied.

I looked at Rico and wondered how he did it; how he hung in there and didn't let go of his dream. It had been such a long haul. Within days of making it to the big leagues, he hurt his knee and was sent home from camp. It was disappointing for the whole family, and even the entire neighborhood. And Rico knew it. After making it through months of painful rehabilitation on his knee, he started working out day and night, hoping for a shot at returning to major league baseball.

"I'll be back at three," Rico said as we piled out of his Mustang. "You girls have fun and stay away from the boys."

"Ha, ha," Rosie mumbled and she rolled her eyes. We all looked at each other and smiled as we yelled back to thank Rico.

"Hey, isn't that Andy Maggiano?" Angel asked as she looked in the distance to her right.

It was Andy all right. I could spot his hypnotizing blue-green eyes anywhere. My heart dropped at the sight of the superstar, even though I would have bet my week's allowance that he didn't even know my first name.

"Isn't that him, Molly?" Penny asked, and she flashed a mischievous grin that no one else caught.

"Um, yeah," I stuttered and my eyes shot her a dirty look. I would have been totally humiliated if my best friend revealed to anyone my biggest secret. "I think that's him."

"He's so cute," Angel said.

"Uh-huh," Penny added and she smiled at me.

I panicked inside. My eyes began to water, and I dropped my head down. Penny stopped smiling when she saw the tears well in my eyes, and she let me be.

As we waited in line, I reluctantly looked up to see if anyone was with Andy. I imagined him holding hands with a skinny blonde. But all I could see were Mike and Monte. And all three of them were walking right through the doors of the same show that we were going to. My palms began to sweat. I hoped and feared that we would end up sitting right next to Andy Maggiano.

"Hurry up," Wil said, and we hustled to catch up to her. "It's probably already started."

We whispered loudly and giggled as we shuffled down the aisle. I opened my eyes wide in the dark theater to locate Andy and his friends. They were sitting dead center. And Wil picked the row right in front of them.

"Keep it down," Mike said in a loud hush. "You're being too loud already."

"Whatever," Wil said.

We settled in our seats, and quieted down for a while. But the movie was so terrible that we wanted out halfway through it.

"Let's go see the one next-door," Wil whispered.

"Shhhh!" Monte hushed.

"Come on," Angel said, "let's go."

I didn't want to do it. The humiliation of getting tossed from the theater while being in the vicinity of Andy would be far too great, but I had no choice. My friends pushed me up the aisle and out in the hallway. We slipped right past one usher and into the next theater.

We finished watching the second half of another movie, even though we were totally lost as to what was going on. But the movie didn't matter. Sneaking from one theater to another alone made the trip worthwhile. The story that six girls skipped from one theater to the next without getting caught would be rehashed for weeks.

"Nobody even saw us do it!" Wil raved as we stood on the sidewalk.

"The usher was talking to that girl, and his head was turned. It was perfect timing!" Angel added.

We stood amazed by ourselves as we waited on the street corner for Rico. I felt a tug on my shirt. I looked down and it was Rosie. I followed her eyes. She was staring at a pack of loud girls dressed up in tight tank tops and jean shorts. It was the Hawks. They were coming right at us.

"Uh-oh," Wil muttered. "Here we go again."

"Well, well," Tasha drawled as she grew nearer. "What are you doin' in our neighborhood?"

No one answered.

"And who's this little girl?" Tasha said and she walked up to Jane.

I pushed Jane aside and stared viciously into Tasha's eyes. We were eyeball to eyeball. Toe to toe.

"Don't do it, Molly," Penny warned. "Remember what your dad said."

"What did your daddy say, Red?" Tasha asked.

I was so angry and embarrassed that I couldn't even speak.

"He said that Molly shouldn't be beating up girls like you anymore," Jane said evenly as she pushed me out of the way.

Tasha's jaw dropped, and so did mine. I turned to Jane with wide eyes. *Are you crazy?* She had absolutely no idea what she was getting herself into.

"And who are you, Miss-Goodie-Two-Shoes?" Tasha asked as she brushed closer to Jane. I imagined Tasha grabbing hold of Jane's long brown hair, and whipping her around like a rag doll. *And what about her mother? Oh, no.* I was sure that it was going to be Jane's first and last time in the city.

"Tasha, can't we settle this on the court?" Penny offered calmly. "You already beat us. What more do you want?"

"I want Miss-Goodie-Two-Shoes to understand who she is talking to," Tasha yelled. Her voice rose, and her eyes narrowed. I stepped closer to Jane.

"And who are you besides some girl with a big mouth?" I shot back.

"No, Molly," Jane said stubbornly. "You'll get in trouble."

"I don't care," I answered.

"Hold it!" Penny stepped right in the middle of us. "If you're gonna fight anyone, you fight me fair and square. One on one."

"Let's go then," Tasha said.

Penny took a step back and waited for Tasha's move. I moved closer behind Penny. But Wil grabbed me and pulled me away. "She'll settle it," Wil whispered and her grip grew tighter.

"She can't fight," I whined as I tried to wrestle myself free. "Penny never fights. I don't want her to fight. I'm always the one fighting. Let me fight." I squirmed and struggled, but failed to escape Wil's grip.

The second Penny's eyes locked into Tasha's, a car horn blared. It was Rico. Penny didn't move from her cold stare. The horn blared again.

"Let's go, P," pleaded Angel.

Rosie tugged on Penny's arm. "Don't worry about it, P," Rosie said softly. I could tell by the scared look in Rosie's eyes that she had never seen Penny so upset. Rosie tugged again. Penny kept her eyes on Tasha as she turned and walked away.

"We'll see you again, real soon," Tasha shot back bitterly.

"What was that all about?" Rico asked as we piled in the car.

"Nothing." Rosie said. "Just some girls we played against. That's all."

"You girls better not be fighting," he said. The car fell silent. "You don't want any part of it. Take it from somebody who learned the hard way."

"I hate them," Wil mumbled.

"Me, too," Rosie whispered.

"We just have to beat them on the court," Penny said lowly so Rico couldn't hear.

"Then we'll have all the bragging rights in the city," I added softly.

That was the last time we ever spoke about beating the Hawks.

Chapter Twelve

B *ang!* The back door slammed, but I didn't turn around. My eyes were locked on the bent rim above me. I was on the line in an imaginary game. And we were one free throw away from winning the city championship.

Swish! When the ball fell right through the net, I held my hand in the air as if there was never any doubt. I imagined myself stoically backpedaling down the floor while the crowd went crazy. I felt the steady pounding in my heart and the ice in my veins.

"Let's play," Frankie yelled, snapping me out of my daze. I turned and watched as my younger brother stumbled off our back porch. His eyes remained glued to his red and black basketball, which he slapped down the sidewalk. Out of the corner of my eye, I saw Billy Flanigan peeking out of his back window.

"Bill," I called out, "you wanna shoot?" He shrugged. "Come on over, Bill," I yelled. He pushed open the door, skipped down his steps, and sprinted over.

"Let's play Rod," Frankie begged as Billy unlatched the gate. Rod, which was short for

Rochester, was a game with no rules. It was a free-for-all where traveling, fouling, and double-dribbling were perfectly legal. No one ever knew why it was called Rochester, nor did we understand its purpose. We just called it Rod for short, and we played it all the time.

"Let's go," Frankie said impatiently. Billy ignored him and kept shooting.

"Bill, you're playing, right?" Frankie asked.

Billy shook his head nervously. Rod was certainly not a game for the meek and mild-mannered. While this made it a perfect fit for me and Frankie, Billy wanted no part of getting mixed up in an O'Malley brawl.

"Just one game," Frankie begged.

Billy dribbled around and then took a deep breath. "Can't we just play around-the-world?" he asked.

"After Rod." Frankie said. "Come on, please, Bill?"

Billy flung up his favorite shot from deep in the left-hand corner. He took a deep breath, and mumbled, "All right."

Frankie and I were civil to one another for about five minutes. After I scored my fifth basket, Frankie slammed the ball down. His emotions were unraveling fast. I grinned and then chuckled after sinking three free throws. My brother glared at me and his lips formed an angry line. I drove to the basket. Frankie reached out with a stiff arm and clotheslined me.

"Jerk!" I yelled as he chased down the rebound. Then I hacked him on his next shot. He missed, and Billy got the rebound. I reached up and tapped him gently on the arm as he shot. It was far from vicious, but it was just enough to make him feel like he was part of the game. Billy made the shot and grinned proudly as he strutted up to the free throw line. He made his first, and missed his second. After Frankie grabbed the rebound, he tucked the ball under his arm and ran around me without dribbling.

"Cheater!" I screamed.

"You can't cheat in Rod, dummy!" he screamed and then he laughed. He finally heaved a shot up. I got the rebound, and Frankie jumped on my back. I turned around and shoved him in the chest.

"You stink!" Frankie screamed, and he punched me back.

Something in my mind clicked. *What was I doing?* I quickly recalled my father's policy about fighting. I was walking on thin ice. Frankie was a wimp with a big mouth.

"Jerk!" he screamed.

I had to start easing up, so I nailed him with a soft elbow.

"That's not fair," he screamed.

"Yes, it is," I said. "This is Rod, remember?"

Frankie's blue eyes blazed with anger and hurt. He was about to cry, and I had to undo all of the damage I had done before it was too late. If I pushed him too far, he would up and run into the house, bawling his eyes out, and tattle on me to Mom. Mom would tell Dad; and then I would be confined to my bedroom indefinitely.

All Frankie needed was some confidence. So I purposely missed the next two shots, and roughed up Billy a little bit. Then Frankie scored again. "You can't stop me," he bragged.

I let him go by me two more times and foul me when the ball was in my hands. I had to make sure Frankie thought he won the physical part of the game even though I was the first person to reach 21 points.

"Let's play again," he said after I scored my last point.

"No," I said, "I got a game tonight, Frank."

"Wimp!" he said. "You're just scared."

I let it slide, and he eventually stopped bugging me. He shot around for a couple more minutes, and then went in the house.

"Who are you playing tonight?" Billy asked.

"A team from the West Side."

"Are they any good?"

"They're OK. But we're playing without Penny. She's at her grandmother's for the weekend."

Billy's eyes grew wide with concern. He knew what that meant for us.

"Let's shoot some more," I said to break the silence.

We played our favorite shooting games until Billy's mom called him in for supper.

"Good luck tonight, Molly," he said as he skipped up the stairs into his house.

After Billy went inside, I started to think about the game. There wasn't a player around who could do what Penny did on the basketball court. I began to wonder if we could do it without her.

I went inside and grabbed a slice of pizza off the table. My dad sat down with Annie and me after he had changed out of his work clothes. He noticed that I was unusually quiet.

"We'll be fine without Penny," he said. "There's no sense in getting all worked up about it."

I didn't say anything.

"I'll play if you need me," Annie said seriously.

"Maybe next time, Annie," my dad said with amusement in his eyes, "but thanks for the offer."

On the way to the game, nobody talked about Penny's absence. But during warm-ups, the gym began to feel empty without her doing fancy moves through the lay-up line.

"Let's go, Ballplayers!" Wil shouted. She ran through the lines, slapping everyone's hands to shake us out of our emotionless trance.

"Nice shot, Angel!" Rosie cheered. Our passes soon became crisper, and we let go of our shots with ease. Suddenly, our focus had reappeared. Our enthusiasm was just where our leader had expected it to be, with or without her present. *We can do this!* I ran through the lines with butterflies fluttering in my stomach.

We won the opening tap. Anita pulled down one of Rosie's misses and put it back for two points. The West Side came charging back, and they ran off six straight points.

"Come on, girls!" my dad hollered.

We needed to get our act together—fast.

"Let's go!" I yelled madly.

I stole the ball and scored at the other end. Wil dove out of bounds into the bleachers to save another. The referee called it out on Wil, but the effort gave us a great lift.

"Way to work, Wil!" my dad yelled.

Instead of pressing on every shot or move, I patiently let the game flow. As it unfolded, I found myself sinking easy shots as if I were all alone in my backyard.

"Way to play, Molly!" my dad hollered as we jogged into the locker room at half-time. We were only up by two points, but we had put together a solid half of the game. *We can do this!* I looked around in the eyes of my teammates, and saw that they believed it, too.

In the second half, I dove for every loose ball, and scrapped for every rebound. I did whatever I could to contribute and I cheered wildly for every extra effort my teammates threw forth.

When the final buzzer sounded, my father couldn't stop smiling. We won the game 38-25.

"You all have a ton of heart," he said, "and there is nothing that makes me happier than seeing you go all out and play that hard."

He came up to me after we celebrated our team victory. "I knew you had it in you, Molls," he said, and I smiled. "You just gotta have that type of determination and confidence all of the time."

• • • •

Later that night, my mother stepped inside my bedroom doorway.

"You were all over the floor out there tonight, Molly," she said with a proud smile. She had gotten out of work early that night to catch the second half of the game. "Now let me take a look at those knees." She walked into the room, and crouched down in front of me as I plopped down on the bed. I glanced at my raspberry-and purple-colored knees. Blood oozed out from underneath an old scab.

"Hit the shower," she said as she shook her head. "I tell you all the time to wear your knee pads, but you just don't listen."

I went in the bathroom, undressed and stepped into the shower. The hot water stung my floor burns, and my body grew weak in the heat. I felt a funny twitch in my leg muscle.

"Hurry up!" Kevin screamed from outside the door.

"All right!" I hollered back.

I shut the water off and dried my bright pink body off. I brushed through my wet curls, and then wrapped a towel around my head. I felt the twitch in my leg again.

I didn't even give myself a chance to think over our game that night. I fell asleep the second my head hit the pillow. In the middle of the night, my eyes popped open and my heart stopped. I withered around in my bed grabbing the back of my left leg. Half-asleep, I thought someone was stabbing me with a knife. When I realized that no one was there, I wrestled with my own leg in hope that whatever was happening would stop soon. I stuck my face in my pillow to muffle my scream. I didn't want to scare Annie. The muscle tightened, twisted, relaxed, and curled up again. I broke a sweat trying to tame it.

Finally, after a long and exhausting 10 or 20 seconds, my body returned to normal, and I fell back asleep. When I woke up in the morning, I moved slowly, and carefully set my feet on the floor. I didn't want to trigger another attack. I tip-toed out to the kitchen and sat down at the table. I stared blankly at my mother as she sipped her coffee.

"What's the matter, Molly?" She looked at me and put her hand on my forehead. "Don't you feel well?"

"I feel fine now. But last night I got this awful, terrible pain in my leg. It woke me up out of a dead sleep. And it hurt so bad."

"That always happened to me when I was pregnant with you kids," she said.

This confused me. I wanted to blurt out something in defense of not being pregnant. But I always tried to avoid such issues in fear she would talk about things I really didn't want to hear about from my mother.

"So what are you saying?" I asked seriously.

My mom took one look at me and laughed hysterically. "I'm sorry, Molly," she said. "I didn't mean to say it that way. They're growing pains for you right now. Every kid gets them. And adults sometimes, too."

I breathed a sigh of relief. "Does this mean that it's going to happen again?" I asked.

"Probably," she said still smiling.

"Well, what should I do when I get an attack?"

"An attack?" she said. "It's not an attack. It's just a cramp. Just try and massage your muscle and work through the pain until it loosens up. You were just really tired after last night's game. Your body overworked itself."

After my mom explained this to me, I ate some breakfast and changed my clothes. Just as I was heading out the door, my mother called out from the kitchen.

"Molly," she said. "Just make sure you stretch out. Stretch those muscles. Did you hear me?"

"Yep," I said. "I will."

Chapter Thirteen

My sister and I were right in the middle of a movie on Saturday night when the phone rang. Annie jumped up and answered it.

"Molly," she said, "it's Penny."

"Hello," I said.

"Did we win?" Penny blurted out.

"Yep," I replied, "by 13."

"Good," she said and she breathed a sigh of relief. "I just got in and I had to know. It's been bugging me all day. I tried calling you last night but the line was busy. I knew you could do it."

"When are you gonna be back?" I asked.

"Late Sunday night. I'll meet you at the park on Monday around noon. Call Wil and tell her, too."

"See you Monday, P," I said and then I hung up the phone.

• • • •

On Monday morning, I walked into the kitchen and poured milk into a bowl of cereal. As I was eating, I glanced at a piece of paper on the table. It had my name on it and was written in my mother's handwriting. I moaned as I read my list of chores. I looked up at Annie as she walked into the kitchen.

"Annie," I asked excitedly, "you wanna help me unload the dishwasher?"

"No," she said bluntly. "I already cleaned my side of the room. That's all I had to do."

"Please," I asked in a friendly tone. She shook her head as she pranced right past me and out of the kitchen.

I sighed helplessly, and then began my duties. I unloaded the dishwasher, cleaned my side of the room, and did not go anywhere as I was instructed. Finally my mother returned home from the grocery store. I helped her unload all the brown paper grocery bags, and then followed her into my room for her inspection. She opened the closet door carefully, peeked inside and shut it softly. Then she bent over and checked under the bed. Nothing was stuffed or hidden away. She smiled approvingly.

"Well?" I asked eagerly. She purposely paused, and then took a deep breath.

"Go ahead," she finally admitted.

"Thanks, Ma," I yelled as I flew out the door. Annie jumped on her bike, and rode next to me as I dribbled down to the park.

"Is little Sammy going to be at the park, too?" Annie asked.

"Yeah," I replied curtly. "You know he's always with Penny."

"I just was wondering," she shot back defensively.

"Are you and little Sammy going to get married, Annie?"

"No!" she snapped, and then she scowled. "Yuk. We're just friends." Her handle bars wobbled, and the bike tilted. I jumped toward her. She recovered on her own, and kept her eyes straight ahead.

I knew I shouldn't have teased her, especially after I almost made her fall off her bike. I hated when adults teased me about hanging out and playing ball with boys. Annie's lips remained pursed, and she did not say another word.

"How about a freeze-pop at the store before we leave the park? I have some extra allowance money."

Annie's stubborn silence gave way to one wide grin. "Can I get a green one?"

"Sure," I said. "But you gotta make one basket before you leave the park."

"That's easy," she said confidently, and I grinned.

I immediately stopped smiling when I looked up into the distance. Penny and Wil were throwing a football around with Andy Maggiano and his friends on the sandlot. My older brother Kevin was there, too.

Annie dumped her bike down, and I raced her to the court. "Lemme shoot!" she begged. I made her chase me around and then I finally gave in. I handed her the ball. She bent her knees, and pushed the ball up in front of her face. It barely hit the net.

"Looks like no freeze pop for you today," I teased.

"One more try," she pleaded. "I can do it."

Out of nowhere, little Sammy appeared.

"Hi, little Sammy," I said.

He greeted the both of us and then scooped up the ball. He nailed a long shot. I watched him strut over to grab his rebound and then smoothly dribble the ball back out again. Little Sammy was a legend in the making, just like Penny, and just like their father. People in the city who were avid fans of high school basketball said Mr. Harris was one of the all-time best players in the city.

Annie chased down one of little Sammy's shots. Then she heaved up another airball.

"Ugh!" she grumbled. "I can't do it!"

"Nice try," little Sammy said. "You can do it. It's easy. Watch."

Little Sammy swished another one and then handed Annie the ball for her try. I glanced over to my friends once, and looked away quickly. There was no way I was going over to the sandlot while Andy was there.

"Come here, Molly," Penny shouted and she waved me over. I pretended not to hear her.

"Molly!" she screamed.

I had to turn; otherwise it would have looked like I was in some kind of dazed fog. She waved me over again. Rosie did, too. I was furious. I forced out a weak smile. Annie and little Sammy were playing a game of their own by now, so I had no legitimate excuse to stay.

I walked slowly over to the group, taking slow, deep breaths. I figured by then that Penny had already leaked my secret to Wil, and Wil had told J.J., and J.J. had blabbed it to everyone else, including Andy Maggiano. If all that had happened, I knew my brother Kevin would eventually find out. And if he ever heard that I had a crush on one of his friends, he would say, "You're such a girl."

I was a girl. And I was proud of being a girl. But I hated when my brother called me a girl.

Just as I lifted my eyes up, Penny let the football go. I dropped my basketball and easily plucked the ball out of the air. Catching a football was always a piece of cake for me. Throwing, however, was a different story.

"Pass it back," Wil called out, and she threw her arms up.

I took one look at the leather, wrapped my fingers around the dirty threads and rolled my eyes. *I can't do this!* I dropped the ball down to my side. I wanted so badly to just run up to Wil and hand her the stupid thing.

"Throw it!" Penny yelled.

I took a deep breath, and ignored all the eyes that had fallen upon me. I wound up and flung it. The ball flopped back and forth pathetically just before it finally reached Penny. I glanced over to my brother Kevin, who had spent hours trying to teach me how to throw that darn thing. He just shook his head hopelessly. "You're such a girl," he mumbled. I glared at him and then turned away.

Penny tossed the ball to Andy. He caught it effortlessly, and then lofted the ball at me. I looked the spiral right into my jittery hands, and bobbled it before it stuck.

"Let's play," J.J. called out.

"Tackle or touch?" Kevin asked.

"Tackle," J.J. said.

"No," Wil said. "Not tackle."

"Wimp!" J.J. muttered.

"I'm not playing then," Wil said.

"Let's just play touch." Penny said. "If Wil doesn't play the teams won't be even."

"Fine," J.J. said and he clicked his tongue.

Penny and Mike split up into teams. When Penny purposely put me on Andy's team, I refused to look at her. Our team huddled up, and Mike called out to be quarterback. Andy, J.J., and I lined up next to him as receivers, and Wil took over all offensive line duties.

Mike didn't even look my way. Almost all of his passes sailed in the direction of Andy, whose soft hands caught them all. The rumor around the city was that Andy Maggiano was going to make the varsity football team as a freshman. And I could see why. He ran around like he had springs in his legs. And after every catch, Andy flashed his perfect teeth to everyone.

I quickly got tired of watching Andy.

"I was open," I muttered to Mike.

"So was Andy," he shot back at me.

"Throw it to me!" I insisted.

I got along with Mike most of the time, so I let this slide without blasting him with a rotten name. I decided to keep my cool—but I could never really keep my cool. Whenever I was open, I jumped up and down and waved my arms around and screamed "Mike, Mike, Mike! I'm open! I'm open!" But all Mike saw and heard was Andy.

The score was 14-7. We were down. I trudged into the huddle with the rest of my team knowing we weren't really playing as a team. We were a one-man show. We needed a touchdown badly, and the last few passes Mike threw fell far off the mark.

"Can I play QB for a while?" Andy's low voice settled me down. Even though I was mad at him for making so many spectacular catches, I couldn't help but notice how quiet and polite he always was. "Just for a couple plays?" he prodded.

Mike agreed. Andy diagrammed a play on his T-shirt, and we broke from the huddle. Wil hiked Andy the ball. He backed up in the pocket, and his eyes locked into mine as I slanted right across the middle. I reached up, clutched the ball tightly and pulled it into my chest. Then I felt two hands slap me on the back.

"Nice catch," Andy said, sounding clearly impressed. He connected with me on the next play as well. From then on out, almost every other pass was thrown my way.

"Next touchdown wins!" Penny shouted, and she received no argument.

The game was tied, 14-14. On our fourth down, we desperately needed one completed pass. The park rule was that a team had to complete two passes for a first down, and we already had one. We needed one more first down for a shot at the end zone.

"Hut one...hut two...hike!" Andy called softly, and Wil passed him the ball. He looked right, and then his eyes shifted left. I patiently watched him as I curled back to the middle of the field. My brother Kevin raced over to cover me just as Andy gunned the ball in my direction. I stuck out my right arm and snagged the ball with one hand and then covered it up with my left.

I felt my brother's hands slap me on the back. I turned to him and said, "Who's the girl now?" He just shook his head.

"Sweet catch!" Penny yelled in amazement.

It gave us the first down we needed. We went on to win the game. When it was over, I walked over to the water fountain with my friends.

"Good game, Molly," Andy said as I passed him. I peeked up at his soft glittering eyes, which felt like they were looking right into me. I smiled nervously, and then dropped my head down again.

Andy Maggiano actually knows my name! I was still in shock as I walked toward the courts. I wanted to ask everyone if they heard what he had said or had seen the way he had looked at me.

Then I stopped and thought about it. Maybe he was just nice and said things like that to everyone. I felt kind of stupid. He was just a boy who happened to be cute, and good at football. If I had the ability to jump around like a kangaroo, I would have looked good catching just as many passes as he did.

Wil looked at her watch and shrieked. "I gotta go! I'm late for baby-sittin'. See ya later."

Wil jogged away, and Penny and I continued to shoot.

"Wil told me that you played the best out of anyone Friday night," Penny said. "Fourteen points! That's great. Maybe I should go away more often."

"No," I said seriously. "I need you out there with me. Who else could handle my temper?"

Penny laughed. Then I remembered my cramp.

"You would not believe what happened to me after the game that night. I got this cramp in my leg that hurt so bad. It woke me up out of a dead sleep. You ever get one?"

"No," Penny said.

I was confused. When my mother had told me that everyone got them from time to time, I had believed her. Confiding in my best friend was supposed to make me feel better. But Penny had absolutely no idea what I was referring to.

"You've never had a cramp where it gets all tight and you just want to scream?" I said, trying to add more detail.

"No," she said, and she kept shooting.

I shrugged my shoulders, and took some shots myself. I pretended not to be at all troubled by our conversation. But I began to wonder if my best friend was human like the rest of us.

Chapter Fourteen

Before we knew it, August was upon us, and we were in the opening round of the girls' basketball league playoffs. Only the top four teams made it. The Hawks went undefeated, which gave them the number one seed. Their first round game was against Sheila and the Rockford Rockets, who had placed fourth. To everyone's surprise, the Ballplayers finished the regular season with five wins and two losses. Our record placed us tied for second place with our first-round matchup—The Kingsley Royals. They were the team we had lost to during our week of misery.

The locker room was tense. "It's payback time!" Wil shouted. "Kingsley is first, and the Hawks are next!"

"Focus only on this game," my father said.

"There will be no championship if we don't win this one," Mr. Harris added. When I heard the word championship, butterflies fluttered in my stomach.

We ran through warm-ups without our usual giggling and fooling around. Even Wil was almost quiet. The buzzer sounded and we headed over to the sideline. After breaking from the huddle, the starters merged at half-court and grouped together again. We draped our arms over one another and leaned into a tight circle. Every one of us turned to our leader. Penny's determined eyes looked around at each of us. "Stay together and we'll win this thing," she said.

Anita lined up for the jump-ball. She gave me the nod, which meant it was coming my way. I positioned myself and grabbed her perfect tip. I skipped the ball to Penny. She cut across the middle, hesitated while dribbling, and then blew past two defenders for a lay-up.

"Yeah, P!" I screamed.

With every surge we made, the Royals applied their own form of counter-attack. It came mostly in the form of one spunky guard named Phoebe. Solely a streak shooter, Phoebe could either destroy opponents or self-destruct within the starting minutes of a game. When she came out sinking her first two shots, everyone in the gym assumed she would be on target for the rest of the night.

"Molly and Rosie," my dad called out in the huddle during one of our time-outs, "I want you to take turns playing Phoebe. When you're running down the floor, whoever is closer must guard her. Talk to each other so you don't get confused. If you don't let her touch the ball, she can't shoot it."

Rosie and I looked at each other and nodded confidently. The next play down the floor, I jumped out on Phoebe as she crossed half court. "I got her, Rosie!" I yelled.

Penny picked off an errant pass, and dribbled the length of the floor for the score. We ran back on defense.

"I got her this time, Molly!" Rosie called out.

Slowly Phoebe's patience began to deteriorate. She grew irritated by our constant presence. On one possession, I purposely guarded her from the second she stepped out of the Royal's huddle. "Come on," she mumbled to herself as she rolled her eyes. I grinned devilishly.

Phoebe sunk only one more shot, and hit a running lay-up at the half-time buzzer. We were up by seven at the break. Rosie and I had done an adequate job of annoying Phoebe for the first two quarters.

"Now is the test," Mr. Harris said in the locker room, "of who wants it more." He intentionally paused and allowed his words to reverberate in our heads. No one said a word. We simply went back out on the floor and showed everyone that we were the ones who wanted the win more.

Penny blew by all five Royals on the floor virtually every time she possessed the basketball. Phoebe tried to match every point on the other end, but Rosie and I remained glued to her at all times. At the end of the third quarter, we were up 32-20.

Once we took a solid lead, the Royals slipped further and further behind. They couldn't catch us, especially with Anita rebounding all of our missed shots and making easy baskets. Penny led all players with 20 points, although it was our defense that carried us. Phoebe scored a quiet 14 points, and we ended up winning, 40-24.

"Way to play, girls," my dad said calmly as we sat on the bench after the game. It was too early to celebrate. We all knew the biggest game of the summer was just around the corner.

Neither of the coaches said anything more about the Royals game. They were too busy hustling us out of the gym. "Everyone grab your stuff because we're headed over to the East Side to catch the end of the Hawks game," Mr. Harris said.

"Let's go, girls," my father called out, and we followed him out the door.

"Good luck against the Hawks," Phoebe said just before we left the gym.

"Thanks," we all yelled in return.

"Is it just me, or does everyone root against the Hawks?" Wil asked.

The question was left unanswered. Rosie and I sprinted to our car. She beat me to the front seat.

"What did you think of my air ball tonight?" Wil said as we climbed in, and she started to laugh.

"I thought it was a pass," Rosie said softly, and we all started laughing.

During the game, Wil had driven relentlessly to the basket, and then threw her three-foot shot about two feet too short.

"It was a great move, until the end," Penny joked.

"You just ran out of gas," Angel said.

"That happens to me a lot," Wil admitted. "I don't know if anybody's ever noticed."

"No, never," Rosie said pretending to be serious, and we all burst into laughter.

"All right, all right," Wil said.

When we arrived at the gym, we jumped out of the car and scurried to the door. Penny and I waited for everyone to catch up.

"Let's go in together," Penny said. We pushed open the doors and walked in as a team. I looked up at the scoreboard, and there were three minutes left in the third quarter. The Hawks were up by six. We sat down in an open section on the bleachers and watched quietly. Sheila got a rebound and powered back up for two points.

"Go Sheila!" Wil yelled. We clapped and cheered. Penny hushed us up when we got too loud. She was right. Our presence at the game added enough hype to the playoffs. Rooting wildly would have done nothing but instigate unnecessary trouble with the Hawks.

"It's not like they can't see us, P," Wil said. "They know we're here."

"Just keep it down," Penny said. "We don't want to start anything."

I turned my eyes back to the game and watched Sheila scrap for every rebound. She fought like a champion despite having two strong bodies boxing her out on virtually every shot. With one minute left in the third quarter, she pulled the Rockets within two points. The Hawks coach screamed, "Time out! Time out!" When the referee blew the whistle and signaled the time-out, the Hawks all glanced up nervously at the scoreboard. They walked slowly back to their bench, while the Rockets fans created a thunderous roar by stomping on the bleachers.

"Rock 'em Rockets!" a woman bellowed.

The Hawks were down, but definitely not out. They came running out of their time-out and immediately applied a full-court pressure defense.

"Oh, no," I moaned.

"It's over," Angel added.

After running off with three easy lay-ups, the Hawks had smoldered the Rocket's momentum and confidence. With their noses up, and their shoulders back, the Hawks' arrogant facades reappeared and remained for the rest of the game. Tasha held her index finger in the air, and Betsy started taunting the crowd.

"Would you look at them?" I muttered as I squirmed around in my seat. I looked around. All eyes were on the game. No one said a word.

The Hawks went on to win by 10 points, which was the closest anyone had ever come to beating them during the regular season. After the game, we stood up from the bleachers and waited for the benches to clear.

"We've gotta say hi to Sheila," I said and I walked across the floor.

"You better not start anything, Molly," Wil mumbled.

"Don't worry," I said. "I won't. I promise."

Penny and I led our pack over to Sheila, whose drenched body was draped over a chair.

"Hi, Sheila," I said. "Tough game." I felt bad for her. I never knew what to say after a loss.

"Yeah," she squeaked softly, "they were just too much for us."

"You gave it your best shot," Penny said.

"I know," Sheila mumbled. "I just hate losing to them. They're just so arrogant. You better get them in the championship. Just win, and that will make everyone in the league happy." She hesitated. "You beat the Royals, right?"

"Yeah," I said.

"You had me scared for a minute," she added. "You're the team that has the best chance at beating the Hawks. Maybe that will shut them up."

"They got kind of quiet when you got within two points," Wil said.

"Yeah," Sheila said. "But it just wasn't enough."

We avoided making any predictions or talking strategy about the championship. We slowly moved toward the door. I looked up. The belligerent Hawks were staring us down. We kept moving.

"Good luck next week," Sheila yelled before we parted. "I'll be there rooting for ya."

• • • •

As we walked into Lincoln gym for practice on Monday night, Wil and Angel made the mistake of bringing up the Hawks.

"It's all I can think about," Wil said.

"I just want to beat them so bad," Angel added.

"Don't talk about it," Penny snapped. "Let's just go out there and do it."

That was our new and improved policy. No talk. Just action—and lots of it.

The coaches kept us relaxed at practice by running us through the same shooting competitions, dribbling games, and lay-up drills.

"Fundamentals girls, fundamentals," my dad lectured as we chugged through the lines. "That's what has gotten you this far, and that's what's going to make the difference Friday night."

After our water break, Mr. Harris asked us to have a seat at half-court. We sat down, and listened to our game strategy. The talk started with a list of the Hawks' strengths.

"They're big, strong, and quick," Mr. Harris began. "They rebound, they play defense, they press, they shoot well."

I didn't think the list was going to end. *Did Mr. Harris think we were going to lose?* It sure sounded like it. He stopped and looked at our wide-eyed expressions.

"The Hawks are a good team, a very good team," he admitted. "But every team has its weaknesses. Every team can be beat. And I believe we can beat this team."

I breathed a sigh of relief. I think everyone else did, too.

"When the boys come in, we're going to have them press you for the full half-hour," my father said. "We might even put six boys out here to play against five of you, so on Friday night it will seem easy." He paused. "That's as far as we're going with strategy. We're trusting that you girls will play the way you have all summer. We don't want that to change. Everybody up!"

We pushed ourselves up from off the floor, and walked through our offenses. The boys filtered in. My dad gathered them together, and gave them specific instructions.

"Make 'em work, guys!" he yelled.

Eddie, J.J., Mike, Marvin, Sleepy, and Beef raced up and down the floor, chasing and tormenting us, exactly the way the Hawks harassed their opponents. After about five minutes, Beef bent over and grabbed his shorts.

"Can we get a time-out?" he gasped. "This pressing business is tirin'."

My dad agreed and gave us all a quick water break. We finished our scrimmage early, which gave us extra time to practice our shots.

"So are you ready for the Hawks or what?" J.J. asked.

"Yeah," I said, and then I eyed him suspiciously. "Who are you rooting for anyway, J?"

He paused. "I don't know," he said.

"All you do is talk about them."

"The Hawks are tough, Molly." he said. "And my cousin is on the team. I can't root against her."

"I know," I admitted, "but that doesn't mean you can't root for us, too."

"The truth is that I really want you to win. Everybody does."

"Hey, guys," my dad yelled down the court. "We're just going to shoot Wednesday night. No scrimmage. You can still come in at 8:30. We'll be off by then."

My dad walked down to our side of the floor. "I just wanted to thank you guys for coming out and scrimmaging us. You've helped us a lot. And I didn't want to forget to tell you that."

"Where's the game Friday night, Mr. O?" Beef asked.

"It's at Tucker Park."

"I'll be there," Beef said surely.

"Me too," Mike added.

My anxious nerves tingled.

Chapter Fifteen

On Friday morning, I rubbed my sleepy eyes as I stepped into the bathroom. A crooked sign written in markers was taped to the mirror.

I could tell by the shaky handwriting that it was the art of Annie. I smiled as I brushed my teeth. When I walked into the kitchen and pulled out a box of my favorite cereal, I found another sign.

The trail of signs ran along the living room walls all the way to the front door. As I read each of them, I grinned proudly. Frankie and Kevin laughed with me as my eyes followed the colorful signs.

"Where is she?" I asked.

"She probably went over to the East Side and decorated the Hawks' houses with 'you're-gonna-lose' signs," Kevin said. "Ma's watching her."

The front door creaked open, and Annie walked in. She fumbled her handful of markers and tape. After bending down and shoving everything into her shoebox, she looked up at us and grinned mischievously.

"What have you been doing, Annie?" I asked.

"I went to visit Penny and Wil and Angel and Rosie..."

"I like your signs," I said.

"Thanks," she said shyly.

Later in the afternoon, Penny and little Sammy stopped over.

"Let's go shoot," I said. Penny followed me out our back door. Annie and little Sammy stayed inside. Minutes later, they came sneaking around the side of the house giggling. I did a double-take and saw that they were armed with waterballoons. Annie sprinted at me and wound up. Her toss was far too weak.

"Nice try," I said laughing. She giggled and darted away.

"Look out!" Penny screamed.

When I turned around, I felt a thud against my stomach and the water explode all over my shirt. Little Sammy had blasted me.

"You little twirp," I laughed as I ran after him. When little Sammy disappeared around the side of the house, I stopped chasing him. There was no sense in retaliating. I wasn't in the mood for an all-out water balloon war.

"Ma!" I screamed. "Annie's making water balloons in the house."

"Annie!" I heard my mother's voice call out. "Come here!"

"You're no fun, Molly," Annie mumbled as she moped into the house.

Then my mother stuck her head out the back door. "Don't stay out in the sun too long, girls," she called out. "You've got to save your energy for the game."

"We won't be out here long, Ma," I shouted.

Penny and I played our shooting games for over an hour. I moaned and groaned after every one of my missed shots.

"Come, on!" I yelled at myself. "Go in!" I yelled at the stupid ball.

I feared that my poor shooting would carry on into the night.

"You got it, Molly," Penny said just as I tossed up another brick.

I was a wreck. But Penny was as cool as ever. She was wearing blue. Ballplayer blue. Her headband was tucked under her black hair and her sweatbands were stretched up onto her forearms. Everything matched perfectly. She hardly missed that afternoon. I simply stood under the net where the ball kept falling into my hands. At the end of making a string of consecutive swishes, she called out for her little brother.

"Let's go, little Sammy," she hollered, and he came running.

"Do we have to?" he asked.

"Yeah," she said. "Ma said she wants us at the house when she gets home from work. She's coming home early for the game."

"Come on, Penny," he asked. "Just a couple more minutes?"

"We gotta go," she said, and her little brother started to walk alongside of her. I watched as Penny calmly strolled to the gate as if it was just another day. *Was she excited? Nervous? Scared?* I just had to find out.

"Can you believe it's finally here?" I asked anxiously.

She turned and smiled over her shoulder. "We're ready," she said confidently. I nodded my head and smiled as she turned and walked away.

We're gonna win. I had myself so convinced that I could hear our team and fans erupt in cheers as the final buzzer sounded. I pictured Wil screaming and yelling. Angel would be waving her index finger in the air. Even quiet Rosie would be cheering. Penny would be high-fiving everyone in the stands. I would be right next to my best friend, feeling like a winner and looking as cool as ice. I would look around at my teammates, who would be smiling a smile we could hold onto forever. *We're gonna win! I just know it. I can feel it.*

• • • •

That evening my father arrived home early from work and took his time getting ready. My mother had traded a shift with a friend at work, and cooked us a pre-game pasta meal. We all sat down and enjoyed one rare dinner together.

"Are you nervous, Molly?" Annie asked.

I shrugged. "Not really," I said unconvincingly. "Well, maybe a little."

"There's nothing to be nervous about," Dad said. "You all should be excited. Nobody in the league thought we would be in the championship because we are so much younger than everyone else. And now not only are we in it, but we have a chance to win."

We finished dinner and cleared the table.

"Let's go boys and girls," Dad announced at 6:15 p.m. I looked up at the clock. The game was at 7 p.m., and it only took 15 minutes to get to the gym. We were actually going to be early for once. "The car is moving out," he added with a smile.

Four cars of players pulled into the parking lot of Tucker Park within seconds of one another.

"Wait up for everyone else," Penny called out.

One by one we grouped together. Angel had tied a piece of blue and white ribbon in her hair.

"I'm wearing my lucky bow," she said with a smile.

We laughed a little, but nobody really said anything. Everyone was thinking about the game. Except for Wil, of course.

"Did anyone see that scary movie on TV last night?" She began. No one answered. "It was about this lady who had these nightmares..."

I had never seen her talk so much and so fast.

"Would you relax," Angel said. "You're making me nervous and I'm not even playing."

"Sorry," Wil said and her eyes dropped to the floor.

As we walked through the glass doors, a man greeted us. "Hi, girls!" he said. "Go get 'em tonight!"

We turned the corner in the direction of the sound of thumping basketballs. Penny and I leaned on the door, pushed it open, and our teammates followed us in. All of our eyes remained fixed ahead. Not one of us looked around in curiosity or awe. Even Wil was speechless.

"Over here girls," Mr. Harris called out, and we set our bags and shoes down on the bench.

I felt someone staring at me. I looked out of the corner of my eye, and saw that it was Mr. Gordon. I turned and he winked. "Do your best," he said softly. I nodded my head nervously.

We walked into the locker room and tied our shoes up quickly.

"Are we ready?" Wil yelled to break the silence.

"Yeah!" we all screamed with spirit.

"Let's crush the Hawks!" Penny shouted. "Team on three."

We yelled the one special word that had carried us through the summer, and jogged out onto the floor. The buzzing conversations stopped, and our fans applauded. We ran through lay-up lines shouting words of encouragement and excitement. Not once did any of us look down at our arch-rivals warming up on the other half of the court.

"Here we go," Penny said just before the buzzer sounded.

We trotted over to our bench. The coaches gathered us together in a tight and private huddle.

"Would you all just relax?" my dad asked. "I've never seen you girls so quiet. Smile. Have a good time. Be yourselves."

We all looked at each other and breathed a sigh of relief.

"What's there to be nervous about?" Mr. Harris added. "Nobody ever expected us to be here now. They said we were too young, we were not big enough, we were not deep enough. But here we are. Let's go out there and show everybody that after all of our hard work, this is where we ought to be."

"Let's have some fun!" he shouted.

"Hustle up, Blue," the referee called out.

The Hawks were already waiting at center circle. I walked right past Tasha. I could feel her eyes on me. But I continued to ignore her. I wasn't there to fight. I was there to play. And to win.

The tension released the moment the referee tossed the ball up for the opening tap. A rush of adrenaline made me lose my breath the first two times down the floor. The frantic pace by both teams proved quickly that a lot was on the line this Friday night.

Tasha picked the ball away from Rosie and scored on a break-away lay-up. We bounced right back with a give-and-go from Penny back to me for our first two points. Our fans erupted in cheers, but not for long. Dee Dee, the Hawks' shooting guard, nailed a 15-foot jump shot. The roar from the East Side fans washed away the shouts from our side.

"Get it back!" my mom screamed.

"Play some defense!" Mrs. Harris yelled.

The first quarter tug-of-war ended with a tie score of 8-8. Nothing came easy for either team, especially with the referees allowing us to push and shove a little more than usual. I watched Rosie drag her beat up body into the huddle.

"You okay, Rosie?" I asked. She nodded as she blew the loose hair out of her face.

"Be ready for the press in this quarter," my dad told us. "They like to put it on when you least expect it."

As anticipated, the Hawks quickly attacked us in the opening minutes of the second quarter. We slowly but surely moved the ball up the floor, and broke the press without any major catastrophes. When Penny blew down the middle, and finished an acrobatic coast-to-coast lay-up, the Hawks decided to bag the pressure and retreat to half-court.

"Let's play some defense now!" my dad hollered.

At half-time, the Hawks were up by one. We jogged to the locker room, and took a rest.

"We're halfway there," I said.

"Keep it up!" Wil called out.

"Stay together," Penny added.

"They're tired," I said. Of course we were tired, too. But there was no time to think about being tired.

When Tasha scored two consecutive baskets to start the third quarter, she hooted and hollered after each one.

"Would somebody please guard me?" she said after her second shot.

The Hawks' fans followed right along with her.

"They can't stop you, Tash," yelled one fan.

When I heard what he said, I rolled my eyes. He had it all wrong. There was only one person out there who couldn't have been stopped.

"Penny get open on the right side," I said. "I'll get it to you."

Penny cut, and I hit her with a smooth bounce pass behind the defense. Tasha hacked Penny's arm, and the referee blew the whistle just as Penny let go of the ball. The basket went in, and Penny drew a foul on Tasha.

"Yes!" Wil screamed as our fans went berserk. Penny collected herself and calmly nailed the free throw, which lifted us over the Hawks for the first time with a score of 24-23.

"Keep it up, girls," Mr. Harris said to us on the bench. "One more to go. Give it all you've got."

We matched baskets to start off the fourth quarter, and then Tasha hit one free throw to tie the game. Neither team could pull far enough ahead. Time was slipping away. We were desperate for a spark.

"Molly," Penny said, "take your girl to the basket. She'll foul you. Take it on her."

I caught the ball on the left side and sliced my way down the middle. Tasha and Dee Dee shut down my right hand just as I went up for my shot. I had no other choice but to use my awkward left hand. I threw it up in the middle of traffic and didn't even look for the result. But when our fans erupted in cheers, I knew that my flying left-hander had hit the bottom of the net.

"Yeah, Molly!" Wil screamed. I looked up at her and smiled shyly as I slapped her hand.

"Keep playing hard, Wil!" I yelled in return. It took every ounce of fuel for Wil to move her body up and down the floor. And it was that special kind of spirit that carried us right down to the end.

With nine seconds left on the clock, we were down by one and the Hawks had the ball out-of-bounds. We desperately needed to get our hands on the basketball. On the inbound, Penny darted out of nowhere and picked off an easy steal. The crowd gasped.

"Look up!" I screamed.

Penny picked her head up and threw a base-ball pass to Rosie who was open for a driving lay-up. Rosie caught the pass, and took two hard dribbles to the basket before two Hawks players collided with her.

The whistle shrieked. With four seconds left, and the score was 30-29 in favor of the Hawks, Rosie Jones had the game in her hands.

"You got it, Rosie!" Penny cheered, and we all echoed the same cheers. Every one of us believed in Rosie.

She gathered her tired, frail body and took a deep breath. The referee handed her the basket-ball. Her eyes locked in on the rim. The noisy crowd grew quiet. She bent her knees, and let her first shot go. The leather basketball bobbled in and spun out over the front of the basket.

"Come on, Rosie!" her father screamed. I looked over at him. His face was red from yelling so much. "Use your legs! Make the basket!"

My heart sank. I hurt for Rosie. She rolled her eyes and walked off the line. The Hawks fans breathed a collective sigh of relief, and the players cheered.

"This one's coming out, too," Tasha quipped.

"Put it in, Rosie!" Wil said as she scowled back at Tasha. "You can do it!"

With her head and eyes down and a frown on her face, Rosie began to set herself back on the line for her second shot. When the crowd began to roar, Rosie's eyes fell to the ground. She was thinking about missing. I quickly walked up to her before the referee passed her the ball.

"Just like you did the first day in practice," I whispered. "It's no different."

Rosie nodded her head, and I walked away. She took extra time on the second shot. *Just get this one.* The ball went up, and swished through the net. We all screeched and cheered, and then scurried back on defense. The buzzer sounded. We all ran over to Rosie and hugged her.

"Way to hit it, Rosie!" my dad yelled as we headed over to our bench. Rosie grinned and slapped his extended hand.

Nearing the end of the overtime, fatigue had taken its toll on both sides. Tasha seemed too tired to even speak. But somehow she had managed to hit a lucky bank shot to give her team a two-point lead with 21 seconds to play. It was our ball, and a last chance to tie the score. We called a time-out.

"Move the ball around, and with 10 seconds to play, try and get it to Penny," my dad said. "Drive to the basket and get a good shot off, Penny."

He couldn't have scripted it any better.

"Everybody go in for the rebound if she misses," he added.

What? I couldn't believe what my father said. *How could he say it? She's not gonna miss. Not here, not now. She's done it too many times before.*

We jogged back onto the floor. The referee handed me the ball and I passed it in to Rosie. As the time slipped away, we patiently followed our precise instructions. The ball landed exactly where we wanted it—in Penny's hands. She spun and wheeled through the maze of defenders, and then tossed up the shot to tie the game.

I stayed put in my spot in the corner, so I would have a perfect view. When the shot bounced off the backboard and then spilled off the rim, I couldn't believe my eyes. It dropped right back into Penny's hands, where three Hawks collapsed on her. Penny didn't have a chance at getting off another shot. She wrestled helplessly through the defenders and then her eyes fell upon me. She pushed a bounce pass my way and shouted, "Hit it, Molly!"

My body automatically caught the ball. I felt it in my hands, and bent my knees. I let it fly just as I had practiced thousands of times before. The ball sunk into the net and then the buzzer sounded.

I froze for a second. When I realized what I had done, I jumped up and down and pumped my fists in the air. My dad raced onto the court and his embrace lifted me clear off the ground. My eyes welled with tears after he set me down.

"You did it!" Penny yelled as she came running at me.

"Yes!" Rosie cheered.

Wil hugged me so hard, she knocked me over, and then Penny and the rest of the team fell on top of us. So much for being cool, calm, and collected.

"Take it easy, girls," Mr. Harris called out. "We still gotta finish the game. It's not over yet."

It was the first double-overtime any of us had ever played. The game didn't seem like it was going to end.

"Let's get this over with," Tasha mumbled at the start of the second overtime. Those were the last words I heard from her. Both teams were too exhausted to speak.

We matched baskets in the second overtime, and those were the only points that were scored. It came down to the bitter end again. The Hawks had the last shot for the win. With 10 seconds left, Tasha and Dee Dee passed the ball back and forth. Dee Dee finally flung up a running, off-balance shot that ricocheted off the backboard, and by some miracle, fell right into the basket.

The buzzer sounded. That was it. The biggest game of my 12 years was a thing of the past. We moped off the floor, as the Hawks fans and players cheered triumphantly. Every single ounce of energy we had was put into that game, and we didn't have anything left. The ending was nothing like I had imagined it to be. I wanted to just fall down and lie on the ground until all the pain went away.

"Keep your heads up," my dad yelled over the commotion, but I couldn't stop my tears. "Keep your heads up!"

We walked through the customary post-game hand shaking lines. I dreaded passing Tasha in fear that she would make fun of me for blubbering like a baby, and I would haul off and slug her. Our shifty eyes met. Tasha stopped and leaned in to say something to me.

"You're all good," she breathed.

I waited for a smart remark to follow. "I don't want a rematch," she added, and she slapped me on the back.

That was it. She moved past me and stopped in front of Penny.

"Good game," Penny said.

"I didn't think I was going to make it," Tasha replied. She reached out and slapped Penny's hand. As I watched Tasha smile at Penny, I realized that I had witnessed something rare. For one split second, Tasha had dropped her guard. She wasn't as tough and as mean as she always wanted to appear.

We turned back to our bench and formed our last huddle of the summer.

"You have nothing to be ashamed of," Mr. Harris said. "I'm so proud of each and every one of you." He smiled as he paused. "But you've got to promise me something: that you'll remember this game for next season."

Suddenly I felt bad for Wil and Angel, as if we had let them down. I began to cry all over again.

"I'm coming back next summer as an assistant coach," Wil announced. "I'm taking your job, Angel."

"No, you'll be my assistant—the second assistant," she added.

"Don't forget this game," Mr. Harris repeated.

That was not asking too much. I knew from that moment forward, a day wouldn't pass without me reflecting upon it.

In the meantime, the stands had emptied. Dozens of people walked by our bench and tried to console us.

"Good game," Beef said as he walked by with Mike, Sleepy, and Marvin. "Heck of a game."

J.J.'s eyes dropped sympathetically when I looked up at him. "I'm sorry, Molly," he said, and I quickly tried to wipe away my tears. "You all deserved to win that one."

Billy reluctantly approached me as I sat on the end of the bench. "Good game, Molly," he mumbled. "You shootin' tomorrow?"

There I was experiencing what seemed like the worst day of my life and all Billy Flanigan cared about was whether or not I would be out shooting the next day.

"Yeah, Bill," I said resignedly. "I'll be out there."

Annie ran up to me as I stood up and threw her arms around me. "You did good, Molly," she said. I felt awful for getting my little sister all worked up. I patted her on the head, and she finally let go. My mother and Mrs. Harris each gave me a hug, too.

Mr. Gordon stopped and put his arm around me. "I'm proud of all of you," he said. But I couldn't look him in the eye.

Mr. Freeman extended his hand to my father and to Mr. Harris. Even some of the East Side fans smiled and nodded at us. "Great game," one man said. "I got a workout in the stands just cheering for you girls."

Andy Maggiano passed by with my brother Kevin and his friends.

"Good game, Molly," said Kevin softly. I lifted my blotchy face up. Andy half-smiled at me.

Sheila sat down on the bench next to Penny, and then Jane walked over with her mother.

"That was the best game I've ever seen," Sheila said. "I couldn't handle another overtime."

"You really played great," Jane added. "Rosie hit that big free throw, and that was a great shot you hit, Molly."

"You saved us," Penny said to me. I dropped my head.

"It wasn't good enough," I muttered.

My shot meant nothing to me without a victory to accompany it. Penny reached out her hand. I looked up at her not sure whether I was in the mood for our special best friend hand-shake.

"You bailed me out this time," she said. Then she grabbed my hand, and my stubborn scowl broke into a teary smile.

We muttered half-hearted thank-yous to all those who passed.

"Anybody for pizza?" Mr. Harris offered.

As usual, no one refused.

"You two wanna come?" Penny asked Sheila and Jane.

"All right," Sheila said. "Do you think somebody could give me a ride home?"

"My dad will," I said.

Jane asked her mom, who had already began talking with my mom. She agreed, and we headed out of the gym and to the parking lot.

"How did she make that shot?" Angel asked, referring to Dee Dee's game-winning toss. Everyone shrugged. No one had any answers.

When we pushed through the heavy wooden door of the restaurant, the owner turned to us.

"Well, girls?" she asked. "How'd we do?"

The look on our face said it all. I shook my head. "You're still my girls," she said and she smiled. "I saved some tables in the back for you."

"Thanks," we all replied.

Being in each others' company helped lessen the unshakable load of frustration and disappointment.

"Did anyone see the scary movie last night with the lady..."

"Who had the nightmares?" I finished.

"Yeah," Wil replied excitedly.

"No," I replied. "But we know you're gonna tell us all about it."

We told bad jokes, and picked on each other for two hours. But in the back of my mind, all I could think about was losing to the Hawks.

"We're gonna beat 'em next year," I mumbled.

"You better," Wil said, "or I'm just gonna hold myself back a year in school, so I can play again."

This was a ridiculous idea considering that Wil was by far the smartest kid in her class.

"Nobody in the league would suspect a thing," Angel kidded.

As the waiter cleared our table, Penny suddenly buckled over in her chair. Her eyes were shut tight.

"You alright, P?" Wil asked smiling, and she slapped Penny on the back. But Penny didn't move. My heart jumped.

"What's wrong, Penny?" Sheila yelled and Jane gasped.

"My leg! My leg!" Penny screamed.

Mrs. Harris hopped up from the parent's table and grabbed her daughter's shoulders. Penny writhed helplessly in pain.

"Ugh!" Penny moaned.

I knew exactly what had overcome my best friend. It was the terrible jolt of a nightmarish muscle cramp. After a couple agonizing seconds, her muscle relaxed, and so did Penny.

"Remember when I told you about what happened to my leg a couple weeks ago?" I asked her.

"Yeah," Penny admitted. "Now I know exactly what you were talking about."

I settled back in my chair, and thought for the first time in my life that Penny might have been almost like the rest of us.

"You looked like you were dying," Wil said, and she laughed. "I never heard you scream so loud. You almost gave me a heart attack. And we've already been through enough tonight."

We certainly had. When I crawled into bed later that night, I felt like I had aged 10 years in one long evening. I hit the biggest shot in the biggest game of my life. And we had still lost to the team I thought about beating every second of the summer.

All I could think of was how badly I wanted to go back to the gym and play the game all over again.

Chapter Sixteen

My eyes opened early the next morning. I squinted as I looked out my window and watched the pink and orange sun rise. Then I rolled over onto my back and stared blankly at the ceiling. The day had officially passed. I didn't want to let it go.

I tossed and turned in my bed convinced that I was never going to be able to fall back asleep. I had to get up. I had to get outside and run around. So I slid out of my bed, and tiptoed across the floor. I slipped on a T-shirt and shorts, grabbed my ball, and quietly crept out of my room. Then I went down the stairs and moved quickly through the living room. I carefully unlocked the front door. When the lock clicked loudly, I froze. My wide eyes shifted to the master bedroom door. If my parents had caught me, they surely would have considered me a crazy child, and grounded me for what little was left of the summer. But I didn't care. No punishment could have been any worse than losing to the Hawks. I gently shut the door behind me.

I jogged briskly through the cool, moist morning air down to the park where the comfort of the courts awaited me. I thumped my ball a couple times on the blacktop, and hit my first shot. I chased down my rebounds and ran from one basket to the next. I shot and dribbled as if I were playing in a full-court game. Running with me were the kids from Broadway, as well as Jane, Sheila, and all the new friends I had made that summer.

In the distance, a jogger turned in my direction. As he moved closer, I saw that it was Mr. Gordon.

"Good morning, Miss O'Malley," Mr. Gordon said as he jogged in place.

"Hi, Mr. G," I replied.

"What are you doing up so early?"

I shrugged my shoulders hoping he wouldn't make me go home or tell my parents.

"Aren't you tired from your game last night?"

I shook my head.

"You all were wonderful to watch," he said in between his deep breaths. "Mr. Freeman told me that next summer he's doubling the amount of teams in the league, and that the championships will be played in the big gym at the high school."

I didn't say anything. Nothing could take away the disappointment that I was experiencing at that moment.

"You should be proud of yourself, Molly," he said. "Don't you see? You all won last night."

I kept my stubborn head down and watched the ball as I slapped it against the ground.

"Someday you will realize what you and your friends have accomplished together," Mr. Gordon said. "Someday you will see."

Mr. Gordon turned away and picked up his pace. I watched his silhouette drift beyond the horizon of Anderson Park, and added his words to the collection of thoughts in my mind.

I turned and continued playing in my imaginary game for a few more minutes. Then I stopped and lined myself up for the same exact overtime shot I had made the very night before. I envisioned Penny under the basket with her own missed rebound, and the bounce pass she threw out to me. I felt the ball's bumpy leather surface. Then I released my nostalgic shot.

It clanged off the back of the rim. Still holding my arms up, I watched as my missed shot thumped against the asphalt. I turned my head up to the sky, felt the rain of colors on my face, and paused momentarily to think about my reaction before it occurred. The ball bounced up and fell to the ground again. I watched helplessly as it rolled away.

It was just a shot. But it was our moment. I dropped my arms down and I smiled.

It was a smile that I would be able to hold onto forever.

About the Author

In Wynantskill, N.Y., there was a girl who shot baskets for hours alone in her backyard. She made up her mind one day that she was going to get a college basketball scholarship. Along the way her team won a state championship and she won All-American honors. But during one game her senior year, she tore a ligament in her knee. They said her career was over.

She went onto Northwestern University where she was a three-time All-Big ten selection and an honorable mention All-American. Her sweetest memory was playing in the 1993 NCAA Women's tournament.

During her junior year, she wrote a story about three Chicago police officers she had met during a summer basketball tournament. For that story, she won a 1994 Randolph Hearst Journalism Award.

After graduating, she went on to play professional basketball in Israel. When she came home, she hoped to make a team in the United States. but she tore the arches in her feet.

Now she thinks of life after basketball. When she thinks about basketball, she remembers all her friends who made her smile, and those who helped her become the person she is today. She decided one day that she wanted to write books for all of us to share. But publishers told her that no kid out of college could do that.

In your hands is Maureen Holohan's first book.

Be on the lookout for more books written by

THE Broadway Ballplayers™

Left Out
by Rosie

Rosie Jones is one of the best 11 year-old baseball players in the city. But will she make the all-star team? No matter how hard she works, will Rosie ever be good enough for her father?

Everybody's Favorite
by Penny

Penny Harris loves soccer. When she finds out the Ballplayers have a chance to go to a soccer camp, she can't wait. But there's only one catch—they have to raise all the money in one week. Along the way, the Ballplayers run into trouble, and everyone looks to one person to save the day. Will Penny be able to work everything out?

ORDER YOUR BOOKS NOW!!

Hurry! Send me the following books as soon as they are released.

Name_____

Address_____

City/State/Zip_____

❑ I've enclosed a check or money order for the cost
    of each book and $2.50* for shipping and handling.

❑ *Charge my Visa/MasterCard Account:*

Account #_____

Exp. Date _____

Signature_____

❑ Book # 1 Friday Nights by Molly ($6.00)

❑ Book #2 *Left Out by Rosie* ($6.95)

❑ Book #3 *Everybody's Favorite by Penny* ($6.95))

Total enclosed $_____

Send to: The Broadway Ballplayers, P.O. Box 597, Wilmette,
IL 60091

*Add only 50¢ in addition to $2.50 for shipping and han-
dling costs for each book up to four books. For large orders
call (847) 570-4715 or write for shipping and handling information. Please allow 4-6 weeks for delivery. Prices and
availability subject to change without notice.

Be a Ballplayer!

Join the Club by ordering your

T-shirt now! (order form on next page)

To sign up for The Ballplayer Book Club mailing
list, write your name and address on a sheet of paper and send it to: The Broadway Ballplayers, Inc.
P.O. Box 597, Wilmette, IL 60091.

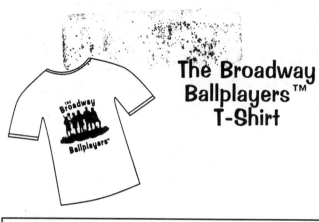

The Broadway Ballplayers™ T-Shirt

Color: Navy Blue Shirt/White Logo
Adult Sizes: S   M   L   XL   2XL

Name_____

Address_____

City/State/Zip_____

❏ I have enclosed a check or money order for $12
   (plus $3 for shipping and handling).*

❏ *Charge my Visa/MasterCard Account:*

Account #_____

Exp. Date _____

Signature_____

*If you are ordering a T-shirt with 1-2 books, the total
shipping charge for both is $4.

Send to: The Broadway Ballplayers, P.O. Box 597,
Wilmette, IL 60091

Please allow 4-6 weeks for delivery. Prices and availability subject to change without notice.

Do you have questions or comments about The
Broadway Ballplayers™? Check out The Broadway
Ballplayers™ website at http://www.bplayers.com